THE EMPIRE
The Mechanical Utopia

The largest nation in the world. With in-depth scientific knowledge and a powerful military force, they perceive those who use astral energy to be a menace and seek to destroy the Sovereignty.

THE SOVEREIGNTY
Paradise for Witches

The country full of those who are possessed by an incomprehensible energy called "astral power." They have been bestowed with supernatural abilities and despise the Empire for oppressing them.

Our Last CRUSADE OR THE RISE OF A New World

CONTENTS

Prologue ············· 001 The Ultimate Weapons of
Two Countries

Chapter 1 ············· 005 The Boy and the Witch

Chapter 2 ············· 069 The Person I've Met

Chapter 3 ············· 103 Binding Fates

Chapter 4 ············· 135 Between the Mission and the Heart

Chapter 5 ············· 171 The Founder

Chapter 6 ············· 185 Iska, the Successor of the Black Steel,
and Alice, the Ice Calamity Witch

Intermission ············· 209 In This Dark Dusk

Epilogue ············· 211 Under This Beautiful Night Sky

Afterword ············· 215

Our Last Crusade
CRUSADE
OR THE RISE OF A
New World

KEI SAZANE
Illustration by
Ao Nekonabe

1 KEI SAZANE

Translation by Jan Cash
Cover art by Ao Nekonabe

This book is a work of fiction. Names, characters, places, and incidents are the product of the author's imagination or are used fictitiously. Any resemblance to actual events, locales, or persons, living or dead, is coincidental.

KIMI TO BOKU NO SAIGO NO SENJO, ARUIWA SEKAI GA HAJIMARU SEISEN Vol.1
©Kei Sazane, Ao Nekonabe 2017
First published in Japan in 2017 by KADOKAWA CORPORATION, Tokyo.
English translation rights arranged with KADOKAWA CORPORATION, Tokyo through
TUTTLE-MORI AGENCY, INC., Tokyo.

English translation © 2019 by Yen Press, LLC

Yen On
150 West 30th Street, 19th Floor
New York, NY 10001

Visit us at yenpress.com
facebook.com/yenpress
twitter.com/yenpress
yenpress.tumblr.com
instagram.com/yenpress

First Yen On Edition: September 2019

Yen On is an imprint of Yen Press, LLC.
The Yen On name and logo are trademarks of Yen Press, LLC.

The publisher is not responsible for websites (or their content) that are not owned by the publisher.

Cataloging in Publication data is on file with the Library of Congress.

ISBNs: 978-1-9753-8545-3 (paperback)
       978-1-9753-0572-7 (ebook)

10 9 8 7 6 5 4 3 2 1

LSC-C

Printed in the United States of America

Our Last CRUSADE

OR THE RISE OF A

New World

Alt hiz orza et yulis bis mihas xel, the laspha et delis fel mihas xel cs.

This world is full of scars, and it doesn't have anything resembling heroes or a savior.

Sera... So Sez lu teo fel nalis pah phenol lef xel.

For that reason, I've become a witch—to drive the Empire to extinction.

So aves cal pile.

Come, divine staff.

PROLOGUE

The Ultimate Weapons of Two Countries

"Surrender."

"You should surrender."

The cold wind seemed to shimmer with white light.

The forest and land were encased in ice. The frigid world reflected in the eyes of a boy gripping his sword and a girl in a brilliant dress, made for royalty. Both made their demands at the exact same time.

"…Swordsman of the Empire, may I have your name?"

"Iska," he replied quickly, tightening his grip around his weapon.

He had blackish-brown hair and a body that made it obvious he'd undergone years of hard training. His face hadn't matured enough for anyone to mistake him for a full-grown adult, but his eyes glinted as sharply as a bare blade. He wielded a pair of steel swords—one black, one white.

"And you?"

"It's Aliceliese Lou Nebulis IX. But you already knew that, didn't you? I'm the astral mage your Empire calls the Ice Calamity Witch."

The girl stood at the peak of a gigantic glacier.

Though her face was obscured by a headdress studded with lapis lazuli, the voice ringing through the forest was crisp and dignified, giving him the impression of a noble young maiden.

They went at it again—

"Did you defeat that unit of Nebulis astral mages all on your own?"

"Are you telling me you destroyed the Imperial power generator for our weapons by yourself?"

Their voices overlapped as they spoke at the same time.

"...I did." The first to nod was the boy.

Behind him were soldiers cloaked in bulletproof robes. He'd rendered them unconscious with a single blow, wielding his blade with extraordinary accuracy and speed.

"What are you? You aren't even a captain, much less a Saint Disciple, the personal guards of the Empire's Lord. How could you have overpowered our astral mages?"

"I've got some questions of my own." The boy's head snapped up to look at the Ice Calamity Witch. "You infiltrated our Imperial base alone and broke through our defenses. And you took out our power generator. You can't be a normal astral mage."

It seemed like an ice age had descended upon the surrounding trees, which had frozen over thanks to the biting ice, wind, and snow. Beyond that were the frost-covered remains of a generator that had been crushed beyond recognition.

The only one who could wield this immense power and create something comparable to a natural disaster was none other than this girl.

"What the hell are you?"

"What in the world are you?"

*   *   *

He was trained to become the trump card of a mechanical utopia, the Empire. His name was Iska, the Successor of the Black Steel.

She was the greatest witch ever born to the paradise of mages, the Nebulis Sovereignty. Her name was Alice, the Ice Calamity Witch.

They were the heroes of the two clashing superpowers.

Now that their paths had crossed, this would be only the first of many fateful meetings.

CHAPTER 1

The Boy and the Witch

1

The prison was dark and chilly. There were no windows or crevices for a stray shaft of sunlight to slip inside. The only source of light was a few flickering candles, and the damp air carried the lingering smell of rust and dust through its halls. That was the state of the cell where a girl was chained to its wall.

Thump. She heard the faint echo of a footstep.

"Who's there?" She jumped up reflexively from her prison bed.

She shouldn't have been able to hear footsteps. There weren't any guards around. It was an unmanned prison, after all. Of course, there were reasons for that.

First, three layers of video surveillance systems monitored every square inch of the facility.

Second, this prison housed undesirables, or those labeled as "witches" and "sorcerers." This girl was no exception. Even when caged, witches were considered far too dangerous. No one could

guarantee the safety of any guards who would have been staffed there—hence, it was left unmanned.

Then why do I hear footsteps?

Who was approaching her? And for what reason?

"..."

The girl who silently readied herself had been born with the inexplicable energy called "astral power," meaning she was one of the fearsome witches. She couldn't fathom anyone creeping up on her with good news.

Maybe they were coming to exact some personal revenge. Or to inform her of her execution.

As the steps drew closer, she did her best to contain her fear and anticipation.

"*Shhh*, keep quiet."

"What?"

The moment they saw each other, he said something that made her eyes go wide.

"I'm gonna let you out right now."

It was a boy. He was a teenager with messy locks of dark-chestnut hair, wearing the battle uniform of the Imperial army. A pair of swords hung from the belt at his hip—one in a black sheath and the other in white.

...Let out? Who are you talking about?

She was the only one in the cell, but it still took her a little while to understand what he was trying to say.

"Don't move. And don't get too close to the bars."

A sword flashed before her. That was all she could make out: a momentary flash of light in front of her eyes.

With one swift move, he'd broken through the prison bars. She finally realized what had happened when the remnants of the bars crashed to the floor and rolled down the quiet hallway.

"…No way."

Even with her astral power, she wouldn't have been able to break those bars, which were wrought from a metal alloy of steel and iron. They would have required heavy machinery to rip apart. And yet, this boy had sliced through them with ease. Using a single sword, no less.

However, the most confusing thing wasn't this incredible feat but his decision to break her out in the first place.

"…Why?" she asked.

"Why? Well, I can't get you out without hacking through these bars."

"…Why are you…letting me escape…?"

The hole was just large enough for a single person to slip through. She rapidly blinked in confusion.

"Aren't you an Imperial swordsman? Plus, that left armband means you're a Saint Disciple… Why would someone from the Empire's ultimate military force be here?"

"You sure are well-informed." As he slid his sword back in its sheath, the boy nodded in a way that could be described only as carefree. "Who would have thought that a Nebulis mage would be familiar with the inner workings of our military hierarchy?"

"…Well." She cast her face down to avert her troubled eyes, which were filled with uncertainty. "We're enemies. It makes sense that we'd study things about the enemy country… Why are you letting me go?" She peered up at him once again.

His answer: "You're about thirteen or fourteen, right? Or are you younger?"

"…What?"

"If you're twelve, that'd make you three years younger than me. Oh, I guess almost four now."

Their respective homelands had been engaged in an ongoing war for over a century. In the Empire, witches were mercilessly

captured and treated as prisoners of war regardless of their gender or age—and yet, here they were.

"I happened to see you get captured, and you caught my eye."

"...?"

"I've got a thing or two to say about the Empire's policy of rounding up all the astral mages, especially someone like you. You're still a kid. Plus, you don't even have that much power."

"...That's just the way your country does things."

"True. All I can do is sneak you out. This is the first time I'm doing this, but if it works, I'm gonna help other kids escape, too."

He beckoned to her from outside the cell.

"Hurry. I stopped the surveillance system, but it'll probably come back online in a few minutes."

"Ah..." She involuntarily yipped when he took her hand.

Wasn't he afraid to touch her? After all, her very existence as a witch was despised. Even if he wasn't scared, didn't he feel disgusted?

"Quick. We're gonna book it all the way down that hall."

His warm hand continued to grip hers as they darted through the deserted passageway. Following his lead, she scurried along the halls with him until they found themselves in front of the emergency exit.

"Go out from here. It'll take you to the outskirts of the Imperial capital. Follow the flow of people heading downtown. From there, use the directories on the electronic message boards to figure out your next move. I think it'll be best for you to hop on a loop bus and head to a city in neutral territory. Here, take this. I'm sorry it's not much."

He pressed a few silver Imperial coins into her hand along with hardtack, which had been given to him as emergency rations for the troops.

She didn't even thank him.

It seemed too good to be true. That was exactly why she'd

started to suspect that this was all a trap. She'd never heard of an Imperial soldier willing to help a prisoner make a break for it, much less hand them money and a meal.

"Now go."

"..."

She was skeptical of his motivations, but she eventually scampered off, propelled forward by her instinct to escape the prison—running all the way out of the emergency exit and far beyond the prison walls.

At the gates around the Imperial capital, she hopped on a bus to take her to lands beyond Imperial jurisdiction. From there, she headed to an encampment where others like her gathered before she returned to her home country, the Nebulis Sovereignty.

She needed to check for herself and breathe in the familiar air of her own home before she accepted the truth.

"...He wasn't lying." She finally realized his words and actions weren't a part of some grand scheme to get her.

By the very next day, word of the unprecedented incident in the Empire had reached the ears of those in the distant land of Nebulis.

"Iska, the Youngest Saint Disciple in History.

"Imprisoned for treason against the nation and aiding the escape of a witch. Given a life sentence."

"No way..." The girl clutched the news magazine in her hands and trembled ever so slightly.

Why? Why would he do that for me, an enemy?

What had driven him to act? She stood absentmindedly in place, grasping at straws.

That had occurred exactly a year ago. It had been a whole year since the incident in question, when a soldier assisted a witch to break out of prison.

Now the world was about to recall his name once again, following a chance meeting between Iska, the Successor of the Black Steel, and Alice, the Ice Calamity Witch.

2

"We have decided to discharge the convict Iska."

The Imperial Senate came to a resolution, united as the body that held absolute rule of the largest territory in the world.

"Raise your head, Iska. It's your first time outside in a year. How does it feel to be in the sun?"

"…It's blinding." With his arms and legs bound, the boy squinted at the rays of sunlight beaming through a canopy.

On a platform in the center of the enormous Senate chamber, he glanced around at the eight men and women peering down on him. They were the Eight Great Apostles—the eight supreme leaders who controlled the Imperial Senate. Of course, they weren't physically present in the chamber, but the hazy outlines of their faces were displayed on the monitors along the wall.

"You don't appear to be in a sunny mood."

"…Half of me is in disbelief. Are you really gonna release me?"

"Indeed. It seems you understand the severity of your crime. As you know, it was a serious blow to us when you released the witch in captivity."

"We've prepared an opportunity for you to atone for your grave crime."

"What do you mean?" His eyebrows knit together reflexively.

When he'd been imprisoned and stripped of his position as a Saint Disciple a year ago, they'd sentenced him to life in prison.

...Why were they discharging him? He'd spent only a year behind bars. And he knew the Eight Great Apostles on the monitors in front of him were not so merciful that they'd let him go without cause.

"Are you giving me a mission in exchange for a pardon...?"

"Very perceptive. You're not a slow thinker, even when you arranged for that witch to escape. I have to give you that."

The Eight Great Apostles chuckled in low voices.

"But I can only fight using my swords."

"You're evading the truth. You ought to rephrase that: It's not that you can only fight with swords, but all you need to fight are your swords."

They weren't being sarcastic. There was a reason that the absolute authorities of the most powerful country in the world had called upon him to give direct orders.

"Let's get to the subject at hand. We aren't going to order you to do something that's a big deal. It's something you ought to do. In other words, we want you to defeat a witch."

"A witch?"

"We received intelligence from a sleeper agent in the Nebulis Sovereignty that they've decided to dispatch a single witch to an Imperial base."

"That sounds...like an everyday occurrence on the battlefront."

"This isn't any ordinary witch. She's a direct descendant of the Grand Witch Nebulis. A purebred."

"A purebred?!" He couldn't help but go bug-eyed at the term. "...That's a formidable opponent."

"That's exactly why we're discharging you," the Eight Great Apostles continued matter-of-factly. **"There was a time when the Grand Witch Nebulis turned our very own Empire into a sea of flames. As you know, those from her bloodline are referred to**

as 'purebreds.' I'm assuming you're aware that incredibly potent astral power resides within their bodies, right?"

"I am. I've battled against them before."

"Your opponent is powerful, even among the purebreds. Her name is the Ice Calamity Witch. During your imprisonment, she broke through the northern front of Yubel alone. It was about a year ago. She managed to steal our latest weapon there and took it back to the Nebulis Sovereignty."

"...She got through the front by herself?"

He remembered hearing about the incident through the grapevine—that a witch with an impressive amount of astral power had made her debut.

"We imagine it would be a tough fight for even a Saint Disciple, especially if you engage with her in direct combat. Meaning the unit on the front lines would be hopeless against her. That's where you come in."

"Iska, you're our youngest Saint Disciple in history. We're counting on you."

"...You mean former Saint Disciple. I was demoted a year ago as punishment."

By fifteen, he'd shot through the ranks and become a part of the forces that directly guarded their Lord. His unprecedented ascent was going to guarantee his status as a hero...or at least, that's what was supposed to happen.

"If you put your mind to it, I'm sure you'll be able to re-earn your position as a Saint Disciple in no time. After all, you studied under the strongest man in the Empire, inherited the astral swords, and became the Successor of the Black Steel."

The floor below Iska's feet parted, and a mechanical pedestal rose up from the ground—holding a pair of swords.

One was in a black steel sheath, the other in white.

"Here are the astral swords passed down to you from *that man*. Take them."

"Are you sure?"

"Only the worthy may invoke the true power of these swords. They are for you alone."

The handcuffs and shackles restraining Iska clattered to the ground.

"From this moment on, you are free. We will prepare a military transport vehicle for you in seventeen hours. It will take you to the front lines. Complete any necessary preparations by then. If you need anything, we're ready to provide it: arms, personnel, funds, rations, medicine. Ask and it will be taken care of."

They would take care of everything. No prisoner had ever been treated so well. When they made that proposal, Iska didn't hesitate to reply.

"There are three members I'd like in my unit."

"We are listening."

"For my commanding officer, I'd like Mismis Klass. For my sniper, Jhin Syulargun. For my machinist, Nene Alkastone. Could you call the three of them?"

3

Sector Two of the Imperial capital.

This was the commercial district of the capital. Within the thick steel barrier of the city walls, this was the busiest area. At one corner facing the town square was a restaurant, Powder Base.

"Nene, honey, where should we sit?"

"Hey, Nene! We still haven't gotten our food."

"Nene—"

"Coming, coming! Geez! Be there in a minute!"

In the back corner of the kitchen, Nene gulped down the final bites of bread she had been nibbling on for lunch. She hastily got up and donned her apron, which she'd left neatly folded, then dashed over to the seating area swarming with customers.

This was the life of Nene Alkastone.

She had her voluminous red hair gathered into a ponytail, which accentuated her large blue eyes. She was fifteen years old and wore a cheerful, lively smile that left an impression on those around her. Her hot pants exposed her thighs, and her tank top complemented her toned body. Overall, this sporty look suited her well.

"Okay, okay. How many people…? Oh!"

A silver-haired boy stood in front of the entrance.

As soon as she caught sight of him, Nene squealed in delight and ran over.

"Jhin?! Whoa, I'm so happy to see you here. Did you come all this way to see me?"

"I saw you just the other day."

"What? Oh, does that mean you're here as a customer? In that case, there won't be as many people in an hour, and the place should be a little more comfortable. Today's lunch special is, uhhh…"

"Sad to say, but I already ate." His voice had a calm and sober quality to it—a stark contrast to Nene, who looked up at him in anticipation with her big eyes.

His name was Jhin Syulargun. His silver hair was spiked up, framing his masculine face and sharp gray eyes. He wore a military uniform that incorporated fiber-optic cables in the design and lugged around a rifle case on his left shoulder.

"Okay then, what's up?"

"I've got a message for you."

"What is it?"

"Our *guy* has been released. He just returned to the barracks, scrambling to get ready."

Nene's eyes darted around, unfocused, as she contemplated his announcement.

"…Oh!" Her eyes glittered as if she'd been struck by an epiphany. "By 'our guy,' you wouldn't by any chance mean—?"

"It's Iska."

"*Noooooo waaaaay?!* What? Really? You're not pulling my leg, are you?" Oblivious to how loud she was being in the restaurant, she cried out.

"You should get ready before you celebrate."

"You mean for his welcome-back party, right?"

Even as Nene bounced around in joy, Jhin didn't change his curt tone.

"We leave tomorrow morning at oh hundred. We're heading to the front lines aboard a military transport."

"…Come again? A military transport? To the front?"

"It's a *deployment.*"

"What?! Wait a sec, Jhin! I've got work till the evening!"

"Give it up. You? Holding on to a decent job? You've got to be dreaming." Jhin emitted a semblance of a sigh, turning his back on Nene. "At least as long as the Empire and the Nebulis Sovereignty continue this meaningless war."

―――――――――――

As night began to fall on the city like a curtain of watered-down ink, a watchtower's light pierced the darkness, illuminating the front of the city's military gate.

Iska felt compelled to stare at the night sky, taking in the twinkling stars faintly flickering in the background.

"It's friggin' cold." He shivered as the evening wind trailed over his neck. "...A full year since I last saw the sun. And the stars, too."

Iska flipped up the collar of his military uniform and let a bitter chuckle sneak past his lips. He'd thought he would never see the sunrise or night sky again.

"Now that I'm free, I've got a perilous battle to deal with. Maybe I'll regret not spending the rest of my life locked up in a cell. It was nice and safe in there... But who knows!"

He dunked his backpack onto the flatbed of the military transport vehicle, where it made an aggressively loud *thump*. Despite the noise, his luggage was on the light side: His only weapons were the swords he carried. Beyond that, he just had medical supplies and a small communications device. If he'd been a sniper, he would have all that, plus his own gun and a case full of ammunition. If he'd been an information specialist, he would have had even larger equipment that needed lugging around.

"Uhhh, what time is—?"

"We have four minutes and thirty seconds until we need to meet up."

Iska spun around to find a silver-haired boy coming into view under the streetlamps. It was the sniper, carrying his trunk on his left shoulder.

"Hey, Jhin. You were a lifesaver today. Thanks for getting in contact with Nene and Captain Mismis."

"I'm used to dealing with your last-minute stuff. Like that time a year ago—when you got carried away with breaking out that witch by yourself."

"Ack... D-didn't I apologize for that this morning?"

"You never follow through. The master always said, 'Whatever

you do, make absolutely sure you will succeed. Otherwise, wait until the time is right.' And yet you still haven't learned your lesson." Jhin sighed dramatically and flung his things into the vehicle. "When you were arrested, those two didn't take it too well. Their reaction was something else."

"You mean Nene and Captain Mismis?"

"That means they're just as worked up about your release. Speak of the devil."

With his eyes, Jhin motioned to the headlights whizzing toward them at a terrifying speed. A dense fog of dust followed the buggy as it peeled forward. The sound of its brakes screeched into the night, shattering the silence. Most of the soldiers were sound asleep.

"Iska, congrats on getting oooooout!" Before the ATV came to a halt, a redheaded girl bounded out of the car. "Congrats, congrats, congraaaaaaaaaaaats!" she sang.

"Nene?!" Iska caught Nene as she threw herself into his arms. "I know you're excited, but... I mean, I feel bad for making you worry."

"It's okay. It's not your fault, Iska. Everything worked out in the end." She looked up at him with tears welling in her eyes. "Do you know just how worried I was about you?! I couldn't eat for a month! Like, I lost over six pounds."

"Yeah, and then you binged on barbecue and gained, like, ten pounds," Jhin muttered under his breath, thinking back to how she'd gorged herself on meat.

"Jhin, how did you even know about that?!" Nene's sharp ears picked up on his snide comment, and she whipped around to look him in the eye.

"...Oh, hey. Looks like the captain's arrived. Hey, over here!" Nene waved toward the direction of the city.

Against the backdrop of the bright neon lights, a petite girl in an Imperial military uniform was hurrying toward them.

"E-e-everyooooone… Haah…haah… S-sorry I'm late…"

"…Running at a snail's pace, as always." Jhin sighed in exasperation.

She was either weighed down by the enormous bag she was carrying or simply lacking stamina. Regardless, she was on the brink of collapsing as she staggered toward them.

"Jhin, how has the captain been? The same as always?" Iska asked.

"She hasn't changed. And I mean that in a bad way."

Plop.

"Oh geez, she fell down again," Nene murmured.

The captain had taken a big tumble, even though there wasn't an uneven surface or stray pebble in sight. But she got back on her feet—at least, she should have, but she chose to remain crouched on the ground for some reason.

"…*Sniffle.* Sorry… I have no idea why I'm so unathletic. Plus, I'm always getting in trouble with my subordinates and bosses. I have to wonder if I'm quite cut out for the military. Hey, Mr. Electrical Pole. You think so, too, don't you, Mr. Pole?"

She started talking to the utility pole in front of her—of all things.

"…Maybe I should quit being a captain."

"Don't give uuuuuup!" Iska scrambled over to her in a hurry, trying to get her to stop making her disturbing remarks. "You can't go home, Captain— Come on, be serious. Who comes this far, then just falls apart?"

"Oh, it's you, Iska." The captain's face brightened instantly.

She was even more petite than Nene. Her face overflowed with a girlish charm and was framed by her wavy light-blue locks. With her dainty, flushed lips, she gave off the impression of an adorable child.

"Whoa! It's been so long, Nene. Did you get a little taller?"

"Y-you think so?"

"Definitely. I want to get taller, too, so I've been chugging milk every day, but I guess a young girl like me can't compare."

"A girl? Gimme a break. You're not that young anymore," Jhin butted in, interrupting their conversation like it was no big deal.

"Wh-what did you say?!" The girl—or rather, the *woman*—arched her eyebrows at him.

That was Mismis Klass, the unit captain. Though she seemed younger than the fifteen-year-old Nene, she was actually the oldest of them all.

"But, like, I'm only twenty-two. And just the other day, I was able to get into the movies on a child discount!"

"…Captain, just buy an adult ticket. Please?"

"Anyway, I'm so happy." With her fingertip, Mismis wiped the errant tear that'd softly fallen from her eye. "An honest, good kid as always, Iska. And Nene, you've become even more charming and pretty than you already were. Even your potty mouth feels nostalgic, Jhin—for today, at least."

"Hey, wait a sec—"

"Unit 907 of the Special Defense Third Division. Back at it again after a year-long hiatus!" Captain Mismis pumped her fist enthusiastically, unaware that Jhin was in the middle of saying something. "And? And? What else? I know we have deployment orders, like, super-suddenly, but what kind of mission is it?"

"We're hunting a witch. What else would the Third Division be doing?" Jhin said dryly.

"What?" Mismis stopped moving.

"Our target is a purebred, a direct descendant of the Grand Witch Nebulis. I'm sure you're familiar with the Ice Calamity Witch, right, Captain? She's been making a name for herself recently. You know, a real big shot."

"The Ice Calamity Witch?!" Mismis shrieked, and her entire face took on a blue tinge. She started to convulse uncontrollably. "I-I-Iska, is that true?!"

"Yes. I was released to catch that astral mage. At least, that's what the authorities said."

"...Oof." The unit captain held her head in her hands. "Iska, the Eight Great Apostles are setting you up..."

"What do you mean?"

"Of course there's no way you could've known, since the Ice Calamity Witch didn't show up until after you got caught, Iska." Mismis had a strained expression. "Um, she first appeared at the northern front in Yubel, I think. She attacked all alone and then returned home without a scratch. And then I think a Saint Disciple was dispatched three months ago, when she was spotted in the Viayle plains. But no luck. There's not a lot of info out there, but rumor has it that she's the strongest astral mage in history. Right, Jhin?"

"On the flip side, our opponent doesn't know we've got a soldier like you, Iska." Jhin slung his rifle case over his back. "I don't think the Nebulis Sovereignty has much intel on you—for better or for worse. Guess that's what happens when you get a demotion right after becoming a Saint Disciple. I mean, you've never even had a chance to participate in a battle. To them, you're just another private. Meaning they'll be coming in without realizing they're opening Pandora's box. That's when you'll attack them with the full force of a Saint Disciple. In other words—"

"We'll catch them off guard?"

"That's probably what the Eight Great Apostles are scheming. But they must have gotten themselves in a real mess if they're placing their bets on a prisoner."

"The Ice Calamity Witch, huh..."

As the wind pushed him from behind, Iska climbed into the back seat of the military transport vehicle.

"Iska, are we already heading out?" Nene settled into the driver's seat jubilantly, ready for a successful mission. She gripped the controls with one hand and yanked the telecoms equipment toward her mouth with the other.

"This is the Third Division. Unit 907. We're on the move! Hey, Captain Mismis, get in!"

"Whoa, wait for me, Nene!" The captain leaped into the moving vehicle in a rush. "Iska, a-are you really going through with this mission…?"

"Of course. This is a big opportunity for me."

They blew past the gate of the Imperial barracks at breakneck speed, and the armored car screeched onto the sandy road beyond. Iska absentmindedly peered through the double-paned windows and watched the city lights stream by. He gave a small nod. But he was firmly resolute.

"…Iska, correct me if I'm wrong, but aren't they gonna throw you back in jail if you fail?" Mismis asked demurely.

"I'm trying not to think about that." He gave her a wry smile. "I'm just trying to figure out a way to end this hopeless war. That's what I was thinking about a year ago, and that's all I'm thinking about now."

4

A century ago, there was a united stronghold under the hegemony of the Heavenly Empire—or "the Empire" for short. They'd prospered at the height of their industrial revolution, right until they came into contact with the Secret of the Celestial Body. The Geological Survey

Unit had found the thing in question—an *unaccountable energy* called "astral power" surging up from the depths of the planet.

Even in modern times, they couldn't fathom why *that thing* had been lying dormant inside the earth. All they knew for certain was that astral power had the capability of possessing humans. At first, it was isolated, affecting only the Geological Survey Unit, which had been showered in the substance upon making their discovery. Then it touched the researchers studying this unknown substance, as well.

Anyone with prolonged contact developed a mark somewhere on their body for reasons still unknown. And the possessed obtained powers straight out of a fairy tale.

In short, all those affected invariably developed an ominous mark and paranormal power.

"…They're monsters."

These girls and women were labeled witches; boys and men were sorcerers.

It didn't take long for the general public to begin persecuting those with astral power, and the Imperial population had grown to fear their immense strength. On the other hand, the oppressed began to seethe with hatred for the Empire, eventually leading them to revolt.

The girl with the most astral power transformed the Empire into a sea of flames and founded a new nation for the witches and sorcerers—the Nebulis Sovereignty. The girl was the Grand Witch Nebulis.

In time, the Empire vowed to eradicate the traitors and regarded their power as an existential threat. Meanwhile, the Nebulis Sovereignty became obsessed with avenging their ancestors and singing the praises of astral power for opening new doors to humankind.

Even a century later, the battle between the two great nations showed no signs of subsiding anytime soon.

*   *   *

"—Lady Alice."

When her attendant meekly touched her shoulder, the girl with golden locks came back to her senses.

"Are you all right? Is it possible you don't feel well?"

"I'm sorry. I was simply thinking to myself." She turned to the assistant behind her as she caught loose strands of hair that were flitting in the wind and curled them around her finger.

The lovely girl in a royal gown was Aliceliese Lou Nebulis IX.

Her golden hair glowed in the sunlight and rippled with the passing breeze like strands of silk. Her ruby eyes were dignified, and her porcelain limbs were pale and almost seemed translucent. The healthy flush of her cheeks and lips, combined with her perfect features, gave her a coquettish charm that was tasteful—elegant.

"Thank you, Rin. I need to stay focused, don't I?"

"I'm sure you have affairs that require some thought, Lady Alice. It isn't an issue," replied Rin with a faint smile playing across her lips.

Her honey-brown hair was parted down the middle and tied on either side. She was properly known as Rin Vispose, part of a family of attendants serving the royal family of Nebulis and the sovereign princess's one and only confidante.

"How much longer will it be?"

"We've passed the border. All we need to do now is reach the battlefield. It shouldn't take more than an hour."

They were flying at an altitude of over 6,500 feet on the back of a colossal bird monster. Whenever the creature flapped its wings, it would kick up a gust of wind, sending Alice's hair and gown billowing.

"We don't know if or when the Empire will fire on us using their long-range weapons. Please be on guard."

"I'm used to it by now." Contrary to her calm demeanor, Alice silently bit her lip. "I've totally gotten used to it... Used to having guns pointed at me and being cursed at as the Ice Calamity Witch."

Alice was the second-eldest daughter of the current queen, meaning she had a right to the throne of the Nebulis Sovereignty—eponymously named after its founder, the Grand Witch Nebulis. On top of that, she was an astral mage who was extolled as the Sovereignty's trump card at the tender age of seventeen.

They were once labeled witches and sorcerers—slurs under Imperial rule. But after her ancestors' liberation, they chose a new name for themselves: astral mages.

"Rin, is the goal for this mission the same as always?"

"Yes. To destroy the Imperial base on the front lines." Rin's pigtails flapped wildly in the wind. "We've received intelligence that the Empire is constructing a new type of power generator for their weapons there, according to our allies in the field. Once it's complete, their midrange weapons will be free to strike at our strongholds without fear of retaliation, and we'll have no choice but to retreat."

"We need to destroy it before they finish it. That should be easy, but... Why aren't we mounting a general invasion of Imperial territory? It would be a cakewalk for you and me."

That was the root of Alice's dissatisfaction.

Even among the mages, she had enough astral power to determine the outcome of a battle on her own. And yet, the most Alice's mother, the queen, would order her to do was to destroy one enemy base or another and promptly return home after.

"I wonder why Mother won't allow me to launch an offensive... even though I'm a full-fledged mage."

"Oh, Her Royal Highness was worried you would say that, Lady Alice." Rin chuckled and put her hand to her mouth. "You

must remember, you're a candidate for the throne. You should be receiving lessons on how to rule as a monarch, not charging toward the enemy. Moreover, doesn't Her Royal Highness always say she would rather have you focusing on your studies in the palace than runing off to see plays and concerts between battles?"

"No thanks. Boooring! I can start my royal studies once we've achieved world peace."

"Of course, I believe there's some merit in that." Rin nodded.

"Right?" Alice flashed her a grin.

But that smile soon slipped off her face. Hardening her resolve, she made a declaration: "First, we'll overthrow the Empire. I'll defeat their country and then create a world without oppression."

The rust-colored earth painted the vast plain below them. Beyond that, they could see the dense forest blanketing the horizon.

5

The Nelka forest.

It was the boundary line between the Empire and the Nebulis Sovereignty, known for its Nelka trees that towered one hundred feet high. Over the course of the hundred-year war, approximately 15 percent of forests in the world had burned down. But this belt of trees had been lucky enough to escape the embers of war.

"…Whoa, these are huge." Mismis's mouth popped wide open as she tilted her head to take in the scene. The boughs looked as if they could pierce through the sky. "This is the first time I've ever seen ones this big."

"Captain Mismis, um, I believe you've come with me to this base before. For a different military operation."

"Oh, did I?" She cocked her head to the side, her baby face revealing nothing but confusion.

Parroting her movements, Iska shot a quizzical look right back at her. "You didn't forget, did you? That was a really difficult mission."

"What?! Ah-ha-ha… L-like I would ever. I'm not *that* dumb. Like I'd forget a place we visited before. I mean, wow, this is so nostalgic. Yeah, these, um, Shuvalts plains."

"You even got the name wrong! And hold on—how could you mistake this forest for a plain?!"

"I-it's a joke! Of course I remember everything!"

"…That was very reassuring."

"It's fiiiine. You can trust me to handle everything!" Then the captain's expression became more tense. "By the way, Iska. This grabbed my attention immediately."

She gazed nervously ahead, where a mechanical engine was emitting a piercing noise and echoing through the forest—a military generator. From the outside, it resembled a gigantic incinerator.

Unlike the regular heavy weapons carried by the troops, which were cranked out en masse, the Empire's laboratories toiled over designing and specially manufacturing a devastating weapon that would be fueled by this very power generator.

"This one's new, right?"

"I think so. It wasn't here when we came last time." Iska looked intently at the machine as he stood next to Mismis.

They were at the strategic base in Nelka that had been established deep in the forest, two miles from the battlefront, where the astral mage units were deployed. But thanks to the titanic trees around them, the Imperial army could hide the existence of this facility.

"Hmm. I wonder why there aren't that many units guarding this giant reactor."

The generator sputtered steam as it continued to run.

Around them were tents and communications sites. Though there were units bustling past them in a hurry, their numbers were sparse for a strategic base—as Mismis had pointed out.

"Oh, that's because—" Iska started.

"Hellooo, reporting back!" A redhead poked her face out from between some giant trees.

"Whoa! …You scared me, Nene. Don't surprise me like that."

"I've handed over the car. I've also found the person in command at that tent over there. When I was checking in, you know what they said? This thing isn't complete yet." Nene gave a few quick raps on the exterior of the reactor, which echoed hollowly. "They're still in the research phase. That's why it's so loud. They really should have been finished by now, but they had to divert personnel to defend the front line instead due to all the recent astral mage attacks—which also explains why there are so few people around here."

There was an intellectual yearning in the back of her innocent eyes.

Nene was a top-class mechanic with an insatiable appetite for knowledge and research. During her time at the military academy, she'd released paper after paper until she was eventually scouted by the Department of Suppression Weapons Development at the Imperial capital.

But she'd wanted to form a unit with Iska and Jhin. If she hadn't wanted that so desperately, Nene would have become a full-time engineer at the capital by this point.

"I knew from the start there was something off about it. It's thrumming too much, and it's making some weird static sounds."

"Very impressive, Nene, as per usual."

"Not to mention the smell and color of the steam coming from the exhaust pipe. Plus, the pressure gauge is on, but the control

ring is stuck at the max limit, and of the seven control lamps, the third and seventh are both on when they shouldn't be during normal operations. In a genuine—"

"...O-okay, that's enough, Nene," Mismis cut her off.

Once she got going, Nene never knew when to stop.

"..."

"Iska, what's wrong? Why are you so quiet?" Nene asked curiously.

Iska's eyes swept toward the machine in front of him. "I'm wondering if a ton of astral mages will get hurt again when this thing's complete..."

To a normal human, an astral mage's powers were on par with magic. And though their powers' properties and abilities differed from individual to individual, it wasn't unusual for the Empire's ordinary firearms to be useless against them.

Iska knew that this special weapon had been made to combat those astral mages, but...

"It's a vicious cycle." With his sniper rifle slung over his shoulder, Jhin was the first one to speak up. "The Empire builds a new generator, the Sovereignty attacks us and destroys it, we lose, we develop an even stronger weapon and generator to counterattack, the astral mages lose, and on and on. This has been going on for more than a hundred years and the world as we know it was built on this endless cycle... Well, that's what the master would say, at any rate."

He let out a long sigh.

"It doesn't matter what started this war. It's only dragged on because of emotional reasons. The conflict has gone on for so long that logic or rational thought can no longer stop it. Someone has to forcibly bring everything to an end—even if they wind up getting treated as the bad guy."

"Bring everything to an end, huh...," echoed Iska.

"I happen to know a certain someone who wants to negotiate world peace. That's an option. Whether it'd work is a different matter."

Jhin walked by Nene before coming to a halt directly in front of Iska.

"I know I don't need to tell you that the throne of the Nebulis Sovereignty has been held by the family of the Grand Witch Nebulis for generations. Their reason? All the members of the royal family inherit potent astral power," said Jhin.

Of the mages, the Grand Witch Nebulis's bloodline ranked highest in terms of astral power. The royal family's ability was incomparable. The Empire was especially cautious of them and labeled them as "purebreds."

"*We're catching one of those purebreds.* Well, in most normal cases, no one would even dare try to do something like that. Right, Captain?"

"Y-yeah… It'll be hard… Harder than capturing ten astral mages," she cautiously replied.

"*Ten?* Try a thousand," the sniper quipped, shaking his head. "We've been at this war for a hundred years. And there hasn't been a single time in recorded history where we've captured a purebred. The Saint Disciples have always had their hands full just trying to drive them away. The descendants of the Nebulis bloodline were out of their league."

"That's exactly why—" Iska started to continue Jhin's train of thought, nodding slightly. "If we can capture a purebred, I think it might be possible to get the Nebulis Sovereignty to enter peace negotiations."

"I've heard this a thousand times." Iska's friend of nearly a decade let out an exasperated sigh. "As things stand, no one in either the Empire or Nebulis will consider peace. If that's how it's gonna be, then we just have to catch one of their VIPs and use

them to force everyone to sit at the negotiation table. That's your idea, right, Iska?"

"…But, Jhin?" the captain butted in anxiously. "If we capture a purebred, then the Empire would be at an advantage, right? I don't think the Eight Great Apostles would offer Nebulis such a sweet deal. I'm afraid they'll hold her hostage, threatening to execute her if the Sovereignty doesn't yield to full and unconditional surrender. That's not totally off the mark, right?"

"That's why Iska has to be the one to catch the purebred."

To work toward peace, the two countries needed to be on equal footing. If the Eight Great Apostles refused to follow through, *Iska would break the purebred out of captivity.*

"He's already set a precedent a year ago. You know, by breaking that witch out of prison. If Iska threatens to do it again, they'll know it's no joke. Come on—how many times have we explained this to you, boss?"

"Uh, ah-ha-ha-ha… Sorry. I can be a tad forgetful."

Jhin looked at her with his arms folded, and Captain Mismis let out a sheepish chuckle.

"As the captain, I don't have any reservations about our mission to catch an astral mage… But I'm kind of scared of those purebreds," she admitted.

"Iska gets insanely stubborn once he's made up his mind, sooo…" Nene latched onto his back and squeezed him. "But it'll be okay, because I'll protect you! Whenever you're in trouble, I've got your back, and—"

"Hey, we're heading out, Nene. You can pretend to be Iska's bride *after* we get back to the capital."

"Ouch! How could you, Jhin?!"

Jhin had grabbed the end of Nene's ponytail and marched forward.

"You're gonna tear the whole thing off…"

"Don't worry. A strand of human hair is even sturdier than similarly sized copper wire."

"I've never even heard of such useless trivia!" Nene clutched the top of her head as she reluctantly slunk forward.

Captain Mismis called after them. "Jhin, wait! We haven't gotten word from the front lines yet. We'll get in trouble if we just go wherever we want."

"I already talked with them. While *somebody* was ogling the reactor."

"When did you…?!"

"They said they had no battles yesterday or today. The team of snipers saw some scouts from the astral mage corps a few times, but they didn't look like the Ice Calamity Witch. According to them."

"…I wonder if she'll actually come?"

"There's a good chance she'll launch a surprise attack on the generator sooner or later." Jhin quickly trudged into the forest, heading to the military transport vehicle hidden in the underbrush. "Oh, and the frontline unit said, 'We welcome any reinforcements. We request a rendezvous immediately.' Goes to show just how much the Ice Calamity Witch scares them. What do you think about the claim that she's a purebred, Iska?"

"I don't think they're wrong. That's what the Eight Great Apostles told me, too."

"It's something you ought to do. In other words, we want you to defeat a witch."

"This isn't any ordinary witch. She's a direct descendant of the Grand Witch Nebulis. A purebred."

*　*　*

"It'll probably be difficult, but I think catching the Ice Calamity Witch would give us enough leverage to start peace talks."

"Well, that's how it is. Nene, bring out the car. We're linking up with the people at the front lines."

"All aboard!" The girl in the driver's seat nodded once and gripped the gear stick.

The thick tires squealed as they spun at supersonic speed. The four-person open-air vehicle jerked forward onto the forest path, narrowly sandwiched by the large, towering trees.

"Raaafgh?!" Captain Mismis yelped like a puppy as she rolled around in the passenger seat. "Nene?! Ah! Nene?! D-drive safely, please!"

"Dooon't wooorry. This would be a piece of cake even with one eye closed."

"Please keep your eyes opeeeeeeen—!"

The front window was shrouded by the looming Nelka trees and thickets. On top of poor visibility, the ground was wholly uneven and riddled with protruding, knobby roots. It wasn't unreasonable for Mismis to panic as they drove recklessly on the "road"—if they could even call it that.

"I-it's been so long. I guess I'm nervous… I wonder if I'll be able to command properly."

"I get it," Jhin said quickly, head propped up in his hand. His sharp eyes glared at the depths of the forest. "Iska is gonna be stiff, 'cause he was locked up for a while. I was out of the unit for some time, too, and Nene was practically half-retired, working a part-time job to make ends meet. Our instincts for battle are nil. The real issue is how we're gonna take on the Ice Calamity Witch when we've just recuperated and regrouped—right?"

"…Y-yeah."

"We're counting on you. This is a perfect chance for you to shine." Iska gave a firm nod to the girl in the front seat. "Jhin, Nene, and me—we're all bad at sticking to the rules and coordinating. But you're different, Captain: You're disciplined, and you always have faith in our decisions."

"That's right. Well, just watch. You leave the battle with the astral mages to us. All you need to do is give us orders behind the scenes."

"Jhin! Iska!" The captain sniffled, wiping away tears from the corners of her eyes. "Oh, I'm so happy. You've both grown up so much…especially you, Jhin. I can't believe you've gotten so sweet in the past year!"

"Yeah, yeah. It'd be more trouble than it's worth to have you get riled up and try to fire a gun or something. Better to have you giving orders than risk death by friendly fire."

"Arghhhhhhhhhhhh—!!" Captain Mismis twisted around in the front seat, swiping and pawing at Jhin.

Watching their exchange, Nene cheerfully glanced back at them from the driver's seat. "Oh, Jhin. I can't believe you'd say that. If I remember correctly, you're the one who told me to 'cheer her up by treating that idiot to some barbecue' when she was down in the dumps about our unit disbanding."

"Oh, did he really? I mean, hey! Who are you calling an idiot?!"

"Who knows. Whatever. Nene, keep your eyes on the—"

—*road*. But Jhin didn't have a chance to finish his sentence.

"Jump!" yelled Iska and Jhin from the back seat.

"Wait! What?!"

"Hold on tight, Captain." Nene sprang out of the car from the driver's seat with Mismis safely in her arms.

From the right passenger seat, Jhin scrambled out, clutching his sniper rifle. Once Iska confirmed his teammates had made their

escapes, he bounded out of the left seat. In the next moment, the vehicle was engulfed in bright-red flames—thick slabs of armor and all.

"Think it's the astral mages?"

Iska twisted around in the air, drawing the dual swords from the belt on his back, and knelt on the ground. Nene and Mismis touched down after him.

"What?! But this is Imperial territory!"

"They've broken through our defensive line. There must be a strong astral mage nearby. Nene—"

"Iska, we have a message!" Nene put the palm-size receiver up to her ear. "It's from the communications team in Nelka: a request for backup from all units!"

"…We can't waste any time. We're dealing with a surprise attack, too, but if the frontline units can't fend off the assault, the enemy might charge in and attack in force."

As Jhin landed, he flicked off the safety on the gun on his shoulder.

Behind him, the thickets rustled loudly.

"Jhin, get back!"

It happened in a flash: From behind, a giant wall of fire caught Jhin by surprise, but Iska used his black sword to cut the burning barrier in half.

"…Did you cut through the flames of an astral mage?!" A man and a woman jumped out from the bushes.

They were members of the Nebulis astral mage corps, wearing silvery-white clothes woven with metal fibers—material that could even withstand a barrage of fire for short periods of time. Aside from the seams, which were less than half an inch, their garments rendered gunfire ineffective. Even with Jhin's sniper rifle, hitting anywhere besides those seams wouldn't have much effect on them.

"T-two astral mages?! Be careful!"

"We can friggin' see. How about you worry about yourself instead of warning us? And don't yell your orders. They'll figure out that you're our boss right away. You—"

"And I don't need you giving me constant sass!"

"Then shut up and get back." Jhin gave the teary-eyed captain a backward glance.

He aimed his gun at the two mages, who were ten yards in front of them. Before Mismis could say anything else, Jhin pulled the trigger with no hesitation and shot them from close range—but the astral mages didn't so much as flinch.

The bullets had stopped in midair. As if time had stopped, the rounds came to rest for a few seconds before clattering to the ground, deprived of all their kinetic energy.

"That's what I thought. That's why you can keep calm staring down the barrel of a gun." Jhin glared at the motionless man. "Acting as a shield for your buddies, huh? You've got the astral power of wind, right? I could tell 'cause the bullets in midair were quivering slightly. Same thing happens when you shoot through a wall of compressed air. Which means the woman must be a fire-type. You did a number on our car."

The two astral mages stood silently.

These were paranormal beings feared as witches and sorcerers across the Empire. Among their number were those who wielded enough power to demolish an entire Imperial building and others who prided themselves on their impermeable defense that could deflect even a hail of bullets. The astral mage corps of Nebulis held the power to annihilate the Empire's front line with a single unit.

"How pitiful. Four Imperial cheerleaders?" The four soldiers could see only her lips peeking out from under her hood and curling into a sneer. "All right. Let's hurry and clean this up so we can take down the next squad."

The ground beneath them started to squirm, then it made a popping noise. As it broke apart and began to fall inward, more astral mages emerged from the hole, one after another.

"Take your pick: unconditional surrender or utter annihilation."

"What? H-how…? When did this happen?!"

From eight directions, eight astral mages closed in—plus the two already in front of them. Ten in total. Mismis paled, blood draining from her face at the arrival of their newest foe.

"Jhin and Iska!"

"Oh geez… Another one with the power of earth? I see. No one would notice you if you're underground."

"That's quite a trick. Looks like you're all really strong."

"How can you two be so calm?!"

"Because we expected this kind of stuff— Hey, Iska," Jhin replied coolly and faintly motioned with his eyes. "About the astral swords that the Eight Great Apostles confiscated. The ones in your hands aren't fakes, right?"

"They're the real deal. I can tell by feeling them."

"Can they cut through *anything*?"

"Once my intuition kicks in again. But I might have trouble with it right now. I'm going to need you to help me."

With his two swords at the ready, Iska eased back as a girl stepped out in front of him.

He turned to her. "Nene."

"Location transmission, complete—" The girl with the ponytail held her palm straight up into the sky.

A ring-shaped mechanism was secured onto her pinkie. By the time the astral mage unit had noticed, gunfire had started to ring out around them.

"Satellite, Star of Tetrabiblos, launch anti–astral power grenade."

A grenade hurtled down at them, kicking up a dust cloud from

the ground as bullets burst through the Nelka trees. After a big blast, light and shock waves diffused in the air.

"Wha...?!" As the surprise attack came at them from above, the astral mages fell to their knees.

Nene had called for the help of a satellite that had been launched by the Department of Suppression Weapons Development. As a mechanic, she'd been entrusted with it for *experimental* use. It was a weapon made to combat astral power, using radiation wavelengths that disrupted astral power over an area with a radius of nearly a hundred feet in two seconds flat.

Within that short time span, Iska had made his move.

"Five on the right," he barked at Jhin behind him as he swiveled to the left.

In a single breath, he closed the distance to the astral mages until he was basically on top of them.

"A lone Imperial soldier...?! You sniveling... So what if you managed to pull off one little trick?!" A mage jumped out from the rising cloud of dust.

A crimson pattern appeared on his exposed elbow. It was a crest—a symbol of those with astral power. Its location on the body differed from person to person, and it was said that the size and complexity of the pattern on the crest corresponded to each individual's strength.

That eerie mark was another reason why the Empire shunned and cursed witches and sorcerers.

"No gun? Are you insane?" The man jeered.

Iska rushed forward and made no attempt to reply. He'd trained his abdominal muscles for years, pushing them past their limits. His sense of balance made it possible for him to maintain his velocity, even as he charged with swords in both hands.

"You cretin!" The astral mage readied himself as Iska drew close enough to engage in hand-to-hand combat.

The mage realized he couldn't escape Iska's charge and readied himself for a counterattack by flinging up his right arm, marked by the astral crest. It started to gleam a brilliant vermilion, causing embers to dance around his outstretched limb.

"Oh, astral power of raging flames, I command you..."

"You're a fire-type, huh?"

"Burst!"

Sparks appeared above Iska's head, condensing in an instant before becoming a massive ball of fire that flew straight at him. Iska was bathed in flames and would soon be finished—at least that was what the sorcerer thought was happening.

But that illusion was quickly dispelled when a fellow witch shrieked at him. "No! Behind you—"

"...Ngh......"

Her warning was too late. The astral mage crumpled onto the ground before he could get a word out.

"The Empire sees those from the flame lineage as one of its biggest threats: They can set a combat uniform on fire or ignite gunpowder and weapons in an armory. But their weakness is that the enemy can predict the size and trajectory of the attack based off the embers. All you need to do is get out of range before they invoke their powers."

Iska stood behind his target. Before the fireball could land, he'd swiveled around, gotten behind the mage, and bashed his sword hilt into the man's head.

"Predict an attack before it's invoked...? But you didn't even have a second to—"

"That's what my training was all about."

"Ngh, don't come any closer!" screamed a witch with a green crest on her neck, thrusting her hand out with a look of anger.

She wielded the astral power of wind. Although those with this power were all lumped together under the same classification, their abilities ranged from being able to unleash a "gust" to being able to summon a "tempest." In addition, there was a subvariety who possessed what was known as the power of dust devils, which could create "blades of wind." This made it difficult to gauge the true capabilities of a wind-type mage until they launched an attack.

But for Iska, simply knowing their element was more than enough information.

"Air currents are invisible, making it harder to react to your attacks compared to fire-types. But…"

He swept past her extended hand, and in a split second, Iska had bent down to her feet.

"It always takes a little time before the wind starts up."

Thud… With his palm, he delivered a swift jab to her defenseless chin, catching her off guard.

"—" The witch had lost consciousness before she could summon a gale.

By knocking out the host human, Iska severed the astral power from its guiding hand, leaving the energy directionless.

In the end, Iska barely felt the last vestiges of a breeze reach him.

The two mages who had just barely managed to react in time had gone silent. The other three had already been downed the second Iska initially passed by them.

"Jhin, how's it going over there?"

"I'm done." Behind Iska, the silver-haired sniper rested his gun on the ground.

As the dust cloud from Nene's grenade settled, it revealed several more mages strewn about, bullet marks on the seams of their armor in Jhin's wake. Despite his limited visibility, Jhin had still managed to land his shots. With his range of vision reduced to a

few yards, he couldn't possibly have seen the seams. It wouldn't be an exaggeration to call his unrivaled precision the miracle of magic.

"Wowie… Amazing as always, Jhin and Iska."

"I had enough time to check out my targets during our staredown before Nene dropped the grenade. Even when they weren't visible because of the dust, all I needed to do was remember their positions and shoot. I could do that much with my eyes closed—no problem." Jhin reloaded his gun as Captain Mismis watched him in a daze.

"What? But you had to aim at the seams of their clothing! That's such a small target…"

"I'm a marksman. Being able to do that much is the bare minimum."

As a sniper, it was Jhin's duty to take out key targets with a single shot each after Nene unleashed her wide-range attack and threw the enemy into chaos.

Of course, it would be a problem if the enemy was able to figure out their plan. What if Nene or Jhin was the first to be targeted? Or if Captain Mismis was showered in a hail of concentrated gunfire? They would need a decoy.

That was where Iska came in—running headlong toward the enemy by himself and becoming the sole focus of incoming attacks. That way, he would draw fire away from the other three in his unit.

"If it'd have been a year ago, we probably could have left all of these guys to Iska, and the rest of us could have gone ahead." Jhin looked down at the collapsed mages. *You're still a peace-loving war nut, right?"*

" …"

Iska had rendered five astral mages unconscious. He'd been on the receiving end of a counterattack from the two mages who'd managed to scramble away from Nene's grenade, but he didn't so

much as blink an eye when he bashed them into the ground. Not to mention, he hadn't used any firearms, which were practically an emblem of the modern-day Empire.

Some called him a demigod; others, a vengeful spirit.

Any astral mage who'd borne witness to one of Iska's charges knew him by those names. They'd seen the way he didn't fear death. But his friends in the Imperial military knew that Iska went into battle while bearing a deep sorrow in his heart, hoping to end the war as fast as possible.

That's what made him a peace-loving war nut.

More than anyone, he wished for the fighting to stop. That was why he would take point on the front lines, restrain any mages who stood in his way, capture the purebred, and use her as a hostage to force the Nebulis Sovereignty to hold peace negotiations.

"Someone needs to play the role of the evil villain..."

Chances were good the Imperial leadership that coveted Nebulis territory would condemn him, and the Nebulis Sovereignty would treat him as their mortal enemy.

"Well, my master told me to be ready to be hated by *both* sides anyway."

Iska turned around as he sheathed his black astral sword. He'd prepared himself for that possibility ever since his master had passed the blades down to him.

"So, Captain. What should we do about these mages?"

"Hmm... I wanna bring them in, but we need to hurry and get to the front line." Captain Mismis examined their foes. Their faces were planted in the ground. "Could you ask the platoon on the base to take custody, Nene?"

"Rogeeer. I'll contact them. We should have handcuffs somewhere in the back of the car. Uh, but it's still engulfed in flames, so I wonder if we'll be able to fish 'em out."

Nene pivoted her heels toward the scorched military transport vehicle and took a step forward.

Just then, a terrific rumbling echoed from where her foot had landed.

"W-wahhh?!" Mismis tumbled over as she raised a small shriek.

It was a roar louder than the earlier bombardment and made the ground rise up before their eyes.

...*Is it an earthquake? No.*

...*What's making the ground move unexpectedly?*

It was almost as though something were crawling underground.

"We're not gonna let you take us in." A girl's voice weaved itself among the gaps of the trees and oozed with anger. "Those are my comrades, the pride of Nebulis. Don't you dare touch them, you Imperial dogs."

The forest ground swelled upward, gathering earth and sand as if it were moving of its own volition. Forming into a humanoid shape, it blocked Iska's unit from going any farther and protected the collapsed mages.

"Is this the astral power of earth?" Nene shouted.

"...A golem, huh. And one that grows fast, to boot," Jhin murmured.

"How curious. You look like nothing more than the average squadron. But you managed to deal with the astral mage unit before I arrived."

The golem mowed down a clump of trees as it finished materializing, while the girl remained perched on its shoulder. Her honey-brown locks were parted at the center and tied back on either side. She wasn't outfitted with a uniform of the astral mages, instead wearing a housekeeping apron and a skirt with a hem long enough to reach the ground. At first glance, her clothes didn't seem made for battle...

"Come alive."

At her beckoning, the earth quivered, and the area around Iska went dark. Something was obstructing the sunlight.

It was a second golem, and its giant fist was coming down over his head—fast.

"Start with him first."

"Iska?!"

The earth around him started to cave in. The roots of the Nelka trees tore apart, flying in his vision as the golem's fist cracked with the sound of a snapped whip.

"—Captain."

The gigantic hand crumbled in a dry heap. Iska readied the black sword that had sliced through the golem's wrist and turned to face the girl riding on its shoulder.

"I'll take her on. Lead Jhin and Nene to the meeting point. Prioritize reinforcing the front lines."

"Wha...? But..."

"She's an astral mage. A strong one, at that. We'll just waste time here if the four of us fight her."

He turned his back on the three and crossed his pair of swords together as he braced them.

The captain was quick to come to a decision. "O-okay, I got it. Be careful!"

With her petite feet, she sprinted across the ground as fast as she could, followed by Nene and Jhin. The astral mage—an earth-type, Iska guessed—didn't so much as glance at the three scampering from the scene.

"You're not gonna follow them?" he asked.

"I will. After I finish you off and rescue my kin, I'll take my sweet time catching up." Her eyes and tone of voice were dispassionate, and she conducted herself in the manner of her predecessors, the fearsome witches ostracized by the Empire in days

past. "So you have the ability to dismember a golem. I see. That's why you believe you can stop me by yourself."

"And what if I do?"

"Don't get cocky with me, footslogger."

He felt something shifting behind him and whipped around to see a fist—the same fist he'd destroyed earlier.

"You regenerated it?"

"It's made of earth. You should think of golems as immortal soldiers, as long as I'm commanding them."

But that wasn't the reason why Iska was bug-eyed: Its recovery had been too fast. In theory, the astral power of earth could be used to regenerate the limbs of a giant. But it was a feat easier said than done.

…To manipulate a mountain of soil at this speed and from such a distance…

…The pure capacity of her power and her skill as a mage are nothing to scoff at!

The fist flew by his bangs by a whisker. With only a moment to spare, he leaped away. As the witch watched him move agilely with the control of a martial artist, her pretty face twisted in disgust.

"Judging by those moves, you're used to handling astral power attacks. Could you be…a Saint Disciple…one of the strongest fighters in the Empire?"

"I'm just a soldier."

Using the momentum of his leap, Iska kicked a tree trunk to scrape off the mud sticking to the bottom of his shoes.

"I'm surprised. I didn't think you'd be able to turn the ground into a swamp so quickly."

She could control far more than just golems. In an instant, she'd transformed the ground below his feet into a quagmire, hoping to immobilize Iska to give her golem time to strike him

down with its fist. Her plan was first-rate, but she couldn't have accounted for Iska's extraordinary mastery of martial arts. Even with the mud clinging to his legs and his movements restricted, Iska dashed around at a speed that far surpassed the golem's.

"Let me ask you something." With the swampy ground between them, he faced the young mage. "Are you the astral mage they call the Ice Calamity Witch?"

"...Heh." Her answer was a scoff. "Believe whatever you want."

The ground writhed under him as though it were alive. Was it a third golem? He readied himself. But his prediction was completely off—something else pierced through the ground.

They were spears made of dirt: Several dozen of these sharp projectiles flew out with tremendous force from the ground.

"Ngrh." He sprang up, somersaulting higher than the golem's head. Iska fended off the whizzing missiles with the astral sword in his right hand.

All it took was the faintest of swings.

As he gauged the trajectory of the countless shots, he selectively took down those zooming toward him, swatting them away with a single stroke of his black blade.

"...Did you cut your way through an astral attack?!" She was baffled.

These earth spears had the appearance of primitive weapons, but these projectiles weren't like the golems, which were simply soil packed together. Instead, they were fashioned out of superhard minerals and lumps of metal. If Iska had been careless enough to assume these weapons were on the same level as the golems, those spearpoints would have easily sliced through him.

But he'd cut them down with his blade—and not in a crude manner, either. The way he neatly parted them into perfect halves could even be described as beautiful.

"What kind of sword is that?"

"—An *astral blade*."

There was a reason why a soldier named Iska garnered the attention of those who held the greatest authority in the Empire— the Eight Great Apostles. They called on Iska for his transcendental skill as a swordsman, of course, and the pair of blades that he'd inherited from his master.

"The black astral blade has the ability to intercept astral power. If I can lock down the correct timing and trajectory, I can cut off anyone from their astral power."

"Intercept astral power? …Ha, as if your empty threat would frighten me. If such a thing existed, the whole Empire would be churning them out en masse."

"They can't make another one. This is the one and only original."

"And you're telling me that some no-name foot soldier is the owner?"

"I didn't get it from the Empire. I received it from my master, the one who taught me the ways of the sword."

"…" The girl looked down at his weapons with disdain.

His story was hard to believe, but he didn't seem to be lying. She'd gathered as much from Iska's unwavering gaze.

It compelled her to ask: *"What's the power of the white sword, then?"*

"You're sharp." Iska earnestly praised her for her insight. "I don't intend to answer. Oh, but if we're swapping info, that's a different story. I wouldn't mind trading for the location of the Ice Calamity Witch in exchange."

"…Silence, grunt!" she barked, opening her small mouth wide. Her face made her fury obvious. "I'll never allow you to even look upon her!"

"I thought you might say that." Iska shook off the dirt on his blade and hounded after her. "But I've some business with the Ice Calamity Witch."

"...Don't trifle with me, boy!" She still hadn't lost any of her composure. "How long can you last with just swords?!"

She gestured at one golem, which crumbled into countless pieces of earth. Then she started compressing the clumps of dirt in the air. After forming new spears, she rained them down on Iska from above. But they didn't have to enter his vision before he fended them off with his black blade. This time, he didn't cut through them. Instead, he aimed to reflect the missiles back at the astral mage.

"Impossible!"

The girl jumped down from her golem's shoulder. For a moment, her attention was diverted by a passing spear that grazed her cheek, and Iska closed the distance between them.

"You're slow." Cutting off her escape, he held his sword to her neck.

"...Agh! Who are you?!" Her face turned red from shock and humiliation as she bit her lip.

She was slightly shorter than Iska. Now that he got a good look at her, she seemed even more delicate and thin than he'd first thought when they initially met at a distance.

Is she around the same age as me?

That musing passed through Iska's head, putting him off guard for a brief moment. He brushed off the distracting thought.

"Tell me where the others are."

"And if I don't?" A smirk sneaked onto her face. "Kill me."

"...Kill you?" he repeated without thinking as he tried to process her unexpected command.

"Strike me down. We are incompatible—an astral mage and an Imperial dog. I'd rather die than become your prisoner."

"Oh...uh, well..."

"If you want to interrogate me, then you can try your best to torture me, or imprison me, or whatever you please."

He had badly misjudged the situation. At this moment, that's what Iska truly believed.

His only objective was the Ice Calamity Witch. If he captured some other witch, the only thing he'd accomplish would be alerting the purebred.

"What are you waiting for? Kill me!"

"—"

He wouldn't make any progress this way. He had to either restrain her, right then and there, or render her unconscious and hand her off to another unit. For a moment, Iska's thoughts veered away from the girl.

"To think you'd actually take your eyes off your enemy... You're helpless!" The girl tore away her skirt.

In fact, it was clear that her peculiar outfit had been designed specifically to let her do so as a part of her battle gear.

"You can use it as concealment?!"

"What? Did you honestly think I would be frozen in fear with nothing more than the threat of your sword?"

Lunging at his sword with the ripped fabric, she trapped the weapon in a tangle of cloth. She used the rest of her skirt to obstruct his vision.

"I'm the attendant and guard of Lady Alice. It's only natural for me to be familiar with hand-to-hand combat."

With her clothes torn and shredded, she was left with what was essentially a miniskirt. In her hand, she held a switchblade, which she'd concealed under the long, billowing skirt that had no place on the battlefield.

"Begone!" She swung her small knife at him, cutting through the fabric of her skirt with its sharp edge, aiming straight at the boy—

"...Urg?!"

He'd knocked her hard into the ground, pinning her down.

"...Im...possible!"

"Whoops, you almost got me. Wrapping my sword in cloth, then trying to blind me while you attack with a dagger, huh? I would have never imagined there'd be anyone with the skills of an assassin among the mages."

She was shocked, still unable to figure out exactly when he'd pinned her down.

Iska put pressure on her shoulder joints, letting out a short burst of breath. "I didn't think an astral mage would resort to a physical weapon."

"...But you still managed to brush aside my surprise attack as though it was nothing—and immobilize me. Who in the world are you?" The girl gritted her teeth.

"I'll revise my earlier question. You just said that you were the attendant of Lady Alice, right? Who's Alice?"

"...!" Her expression changed.

"That wouldn't be the Ice Calamity—?"

"That's my name." Those words hadn't come from the girl underneath him.

Who was it? He twisted around to see the source of the voice that had rung out behind him.

...*Shudder.* This was unlike anything he had ever felt before. He could say that for sure. The creeping chill down his spine was so alarming that he ignored everything else to leap as far away as he could manage.

"I'll show you. Feel it for yourself."

*   *   *

"Great Ice Calamity—"

Psht.

The air, the trees, the ground, everything in his vision was enveloped by a white fog, as if he had fallen into a trance. In an instant, the world he had seen moments ago was encased in cold, glittering blue ice.

"Ow!"

He felt a numbingly frigid chill at his neck and arms. The second a gust carrying ice and snow hit him, his limbs started to shiver uncontrollably.

...Even though I jumped this high to avoid her attack, it's still this cold up here?

...Just how freezing is it on the ground, then?

Clack. He heard the sound of footsteps echoing across the ice.

A girl in set of clothes fit for royalty stood atop a hill of frost, hiding her face under a magnificent headdress. But her voice was surprisingly young.

"Rin, are you hurt?"

"Lady Alice!" The attendant looked up at the newcomer with a warm expression and spoke in a sunny voice—a world of difference from how she treated Iska.

No one would be this excited by the arrival of ordinary reinforcements. Her face conveyed absolute reverence and faith, along with the belief that she could weather any plight or despair as long as she had her lady.

Meanwhile, Iska was *icing over.*

"...This has to be a joke," he spat, his breath turning into shimmering white ice.

He surveyed the ground, the gigantic trees, the thickets around him. Everything was draped in frost.

It was like the coming of another ice age. All this had happened during the few seconds Iska had taken to scramble into the air. How cold did it have to become to cause this?

...If I hadn't jumped, what would have happened to me?

...I would have been powerless, sealed away in a block of ice.

"Lady Alice, please be careful. I don't know what tricks are up his sleeve, but that sword can cut through and interrupt astral power."

"Thank you, Rin. But that's a trivial matter."

"What?"

"If my attack just now had finished him, his sword or whatever wouldn't have mattered. Impressive that he managed to evade it."

The newly arrived witch patted Rin's head and turned to Iska.

She wore an incredibly ornate royal gown. The headdress and the veil over her face were dazzling. Though for a different reason than Rin, she also wasn't dressed appropriately for the battlefield. She was practically confessing that she was a big shot from the Nebulis Sovereignty.

"Still, well done. Rin, you did a great job buying time."

"Buying time?"

"What do you think is behind me?" The girl in the royal gown inclined her head to indicate something in the distance—beyond the icy forest.

"...Is that the power generator?!"

The reactor was frozen in a giant block of ice. It was far away enough to be indistinct, and yet, he could clearly see what had occurred with his naked eye. The impressively rugged form of the military generator had been reborn as an immaculate crystalline icicle. Catching the sun's rays, it twinkled as it scattered the light.

"Collapse," she uttered, and the machine contorted as though some entity was crushing it underfoot.

It warped and quickly became nothing more than scrap metal as it made a thunderous cacophony, screeching under the pressure.

"...This was your goal all along." Iska expressed his regrets.

At that very moment, Mismis, Jhin, and Nene were scrambling to join the battle that was already raging along the front lines. Iska had purposefully chosen to position himself in a location that would allow him to run over and support them at any time.

But the enemy's goal had been to attack the base directly.

"You mean you pushed into the Imperial base all on your own?"

"Is that an issue?" She didn't have a single gash or a speck of dust on her pristine dress.

There should have been reserve units stationed at the Imperial base. If a witch had appeared there, it wouldn't have been strange for them to surround and empty their guns on her. But...

"Oh, I guess there was an issue. Namely, you."

Even through the mysterious veil, he could feel her cold gaze—filled with hostility.

"If everything had gone according to plan, I would have captured a hundred prisoners of war at that base and seized the cutting-edge weapons for study. But I never got the chance. If I hadn't hurried over here, Rin would have been captured."

"—"

"Now, who might you be? I find it hard to believe that a 'nobody' could have overwhelmed Rin. Especially someone who isn't even a Saint Disciple."

Iska's response was in essence a declaration of war. "I came here to capture you."

"To capture me? Who do you think you're talking to? If you

don't want to face an icy fate worse than death, then I suggest you—"

"Surrender."

"You should surrender."

They were in a glittering white world.

A boy gripping his sword and a girl in a brilliant dress, made for royalty, demanded their surrender at the exact same time.

"...Swordsman of the Empire, may I have your name?"

"Iska," he replied honestly, tightening his grip around his weapon.

If he had a record as a Saint Disciple, she could have looked up his history from previous battles, but he didn't need to worry about that.

"And you?"

"It's Aliceliese Lou Nebulis IX. But you already knew that, didn't you? I'm an astral mage. Your Empire calls me the Ice Calamity Witch."

The girl stood at the peak of a gigantic glacier.

Though her face was obscured by a headdress studded with lapis lazuli, the voice ringing through the forest was crisp and dignified, giving him the impression of a noble young maiden.

"Did you defeat the astral mage unit of Nebulis all on your own?"

"Are you telling me you destroyed the Imperial power generator for our weapons by yourself?"

Their voices overlapped as they spoke at the same time.

"...I did." Iska nodded.

Far from him were the two astral mages who were still unconscious.

"What are you? You aren't even a captain, much less a Saint Disciple, the personal guards of the Empire's Lord. How could you have overpowered our astral mage unit?"

"That's what I wanna ask you. You infiltrated our Imperial base alone and broke through our defenses. And you took out our power generator. You can't be a normal astral mage."

It seemed like an ice age had descended upon the surrounding trees, which had frozen over thanks to the biting ice, wind, and snow. Beyond that were the frost-covered remains of the generator that had been crushed beyond recognition. The steel armor hadn't been able to hold up against the cold and ice, leaving it collapsed into the ground.

...This is the Ice Calamity Witch.

...This might be the first time I've seen such a large-scale astral technique.

She was an order of magnitude above other mages. Even if they'd gathered ten astral mages of the same ice lineage, most likely none of them would have even come close to her power.

However, that was exactly why Iska was confident.

An astral mage as powerful as the Ice Calamity Witch had to be part of the Nebulis family's royal bloodline. There was no mistake that she was someone close to the current Nebulis queen.

"What the hell are you?"

"What in the world are you?"

He was trained to become the trump card of a mechanical utopia, the Empire. His name was Iska, the Successor of the Black Steel.

She was the greatest witch ever born to the paradise of mages, the Nebulis Sovereignty. Her name was Alice, the Ice Calamity Witch.

The two made their moves at the same time.

"Come forth, wall—crush him!"

Alice unleashed her command at the ice that Iska stood on, causing it to fissure immediately. The chasm opened wide, tripping

him momentarily, as sheets of ice closed in on Iska from all four directions, fully intent on flattening him.

"...Trying to corner me, huh?"

The walls were too big to slice through with his sword. After making that judgment call, Iska dashed toward one of the fast approaching ice panels.

"Why did he jump at the barrier?!" Alice's attendant, Rin, had her eyes opened wide as Iska crouched down and slid over the icy floor, finding a gap between the walls.

Before four corners were closed off, he managed to slip out.

"That's what I thought he would do. If he could overpower Rin, he should be able to avoid this much." Under the veil that hid her face, the Ice Calamity Witch smiled fearlessly. **"Ice Calamity—Blizzard of a Thousand Thorns."**

"Ice blades?"

Had she purposefully left an opening in order to lead him where she wanted?

Iska belatedly came to this realization when he saw several hundred blades glittering in the direction he was sliding, pouring out from the icy floor, from the air, and even from the frozen-over trunks of the large trees—an endless wave.

He'd managed to avoid Rin's earth spears by leaping into the air. But these innumerable ice blades covered every angle the moment they popped into existence. He had nowhere to run.

"A thousand swords coming from all directions. Dodge them if you can." The astral mage lifted her hand. "Impale him."

From overhead, the side, and below, a storm of blades rained down on him. He had no chance of escaping or protecting himself. What could he possibly do?

There wasn't any room for debate: He would break through it head-on.

Iska readied his two astral weapons and sprinted along the glacial surface. *"Hah!"*

He gripped his black sword and angled it at his side as he spun like a top, slashing the incoming projectiles. He could feel the light touch of some icicles at his feet graze the hem of his battle uniform, but he managed to evade them by a hairbreadth.

He charged forward, deflecting the ice blades in the air with a stroke of his left sword before knocking down other blades. All the while, he fended off the assault in his periphery and struck the blades hounding him from behind—guessing their location from the faintest change in the air around him through his skin.

"—Above!"

Iska became aware of the ice blades in his blind spot, with less than a second to intercept them. But he did it without even looking: The airflow had been disturbed by the manifestation of the ice blades, and he'd reacted instantaneously to the chill in the air.

"...That was something." The one who had spoken was none other than the Ice Calamity Witch herself, looking somewhat exasperated. "But I won't let you go. You must realize that astral power is the will of the planet itself. As an Imperial soldier who rejects its power, you and your swords cannot face me and my power."

Iska hadn't even managed to cut down a hundred of her ice blades yet—but that was already enough to push him to his limits. More sharp icicles zoomed toward him, forcing him farther away from Alice, when his goal was to get closer.

"Guh..."

One of the ice blades that he'd missed cut his right arm as it whizzed by. The pain that shot through him made Iska lose his concentration for a split second. In that vulnerable moment, his left thigh, his waist, his shoulder, and more were grazed by additional spikes.

"You're reaching your limit."

"*Nope.*"

The white sword in Iska's hands began to glow.

He'd used the black steel one to fend off Rin's attacks, intercepting her astral power. And the other sword—

"*Awaken.*"

Above his head, ice blades of the same make as the Ice Calamity Witch's creations popped into existence and hurtled toward her.

"Using the same attack as Lady Alice?! How... How did you get that power?!"

"It's not mine. It's the astral sword's."

It could perform an astral release: The black sword could intercept any astral techniques, storing them until the right moment—when the white blade would "reproduce" them just once.

Iska was bathed in a blue light, the color of lapis lazuli—not by Alice's swords but by those Iska had unleashed from his white blade.

"Ninety-seven. That's the number of blades that the black sword intercepted and the number that the white one can re-create."

"And? What are you going to do with so few? That's far from being able to counter my powers."

"Counter? Bad guess. I'm going to use these"—he wiped a gash on his cheek with the back of his hand and stabbed the white astral sword into the earth—"to get to you."

The ninety-seven icicles, identical to the ones Alice had unleashed, struck down every shot aimed at Iska. As that was happening, he charged.

He ran straight toward the Ice Calamity Witch, who stood in the middle of a world of ice.

His attack wasn't enough to cancel out her attack, but it bought Iska enough time to close the distance between them.

"Lady Alice!" Rin had guessed his aim and shouted at her master instinctively.

Iska bolted up the hill of ice and snow. Alice had been composed and unflinching up until that very moment, but now she braced herself for the first time as she watched him accelerate to an unimaginable speed.

"I'd like to tell you that was a good plan…but it's useless." She thrust her right arm in front of her and snapped her fingers.

Gshk. From her feet, a mirror shield creaked out of the ground—the most beautiful thing in all the land.

"Ice flower."

The sound of a deafening crack reverberated through the frozen forest.

"Geez, that's hard!" Iska's face contorted after he attempted to swing his sword down.

A large flower had bloomed in front of Alice and stopped his sword—the blade that could cut through any astral power.

"An invincible shield: It's even resisted the firepower of Imperial weapons of mass destruction."

"…And is perfect for both offense and defense, huh?"

"That's right. You ought to give up!"

A cold blast from the gigantic icy bloom sent Iska flying into the air. As he tumbled through the sky, Alice calculated where he'd land, then summoned innumerable ice blades on the spot.

But there was a reason the Eight Great Apostles had entrusted Iska with the only pair of astral swords in the whole world, and Alice was still underestimating him—and the sheer *tenacity* of the boy, the Successor of the Black Steel.

"…Give…up…you say?" Iska spat as he bit his lip between each word, even as he was blasted upward by the icy winds. "If I give up here, who's gonna stop this war?!"

"—Wha?"

For a moment, Alice and Rin were caught off guard, and they swept their gazes up to look at him. Iska had stuck both the astral swords deep into the frozen trunk of a giant tree in front of him, then launched himself straight from it, nimbly leaping to another nearby tree.

His practically inhuman speed made Alice lose sight of him for a few seconds. Finally, Iska leaped past the ice-flower shield and landed right behind her.

"Wha—?!" The Ice Calamity Witch let out an astonished cry as she flipped around. "Vines, bind him!"

Vines of frost shot out from Iska's landing spot, entwining themselves around his ankles before he could bring his feet down.

"Geez! You're quite persistent...! Hurry up and surrender or simply die already!"

"That's my damn line!"

Before they could bind his whole body, Iska sliced through the vines, and in that time, the astral mage retreated further up the hill, escaping from his vicinity.

"...Lady Alice is ceding ground?" Rin was watching the scene in disbelief.

Alice could have used any means to pursue Iska as he hacked away at the vines, but she chose instead to abandon her advantage and distance herself.

She had to be scared—concerned about a potential counter-attack if she pursued him.

She knew half-baked attempts wouldn't work on this swordsman. He dodged her attacks in ways that shouldn't be possible for humans, and if he found a moment when she was off guard, he would go straight for her throat. That was why she chose to pull back.

"How idiotic." Her breath spilled from her lips under the veil in a sparkling white puff.

"Idiotic?"

"I'm talking about you." Alice looked down on Iska from the hill.

"You're a beast. No matter how many times I think I've won, you insist on surviving, hounding me over and over again... It's idiotic. You call us witches and sorcerers when you're the one who's the monstrosity."

"...As if." Iska wiped the sweat on his forehead as he answered, glancing around the glacial forest at the strewn masses of ice blades that could have easily annihilated an entire Imperial battalion.

She had the power to level a city and then some. On top of that, her invincible ice flower rendered his attacks ineffective.

"I could say the same about you."

"I'll take that as a compliment. But I don't intend on withdrawing. I won't let anyone get in the way of my goal to defeat the Empire and unite the world."

"...Unite the world?"

"I want perpetual peace without violence or oppression. I wonder if someone like you could comprehend that." But she must not have expected any response, because she looked pleased with herself and puffed out her chest to continue her grand proclamation. "That's right. That's exactly why as the rightful successor to the crown, I, Aliceliese— Wha—? *Ahhhhhhhhh!*"

The moment she took a proud step forward, she stumbled on a hunk of ice and then shrieked as she tumbled down.

"Nooooooo!"

"Whoa!"

The astral mage was sliding down the hill—Iska acted fast.

"...Ow."

"A-are you okay?" Iska caught the girl, stopping her from slipping down the rest of the slope.

"Uh, yes, thank you… I mean, wh-wh-wh-what do you think you're doing?!"

"…Uh." He had acted on reflex.

But Iska couldn't find it in him to string a proper sentence together, because he was cradling the Ice Calamity Witch in his arms. Her headdress had fallen off from the impact of her fall, revealing her face.

"———Huh?" Alice touched her own face, as if she'd just realized it herself.

Her face had been exposed—and it was a vision, captivating and absolutely breathtaking.

Her beautiful features were arranged into a cold and dignified expression; her long, glossy eyelashes and faintly red lips would have made a fairy-tale princess pale in comparison. That was how lovely she was.

"………"

It was exactly as though time had stopped in the frozen world as they gazed at each other.

"Ugh! You *saw*, didn't you?" The astral mage was the first to snap back to reality, brushing off Iska's hand and backing away. She thrust out her hand with a menacing look on her face. "I can't let the Empire know what I look like! Now I can't let you go!" She gritted her teeth audibly and glared at him. "We'll end this here and—"

"Iska!"

That was when he heard his companion's voice from afar.

"Nene?!"

"Oh, Iska! Wh-what's with this ice?!"

Next, he heard Captain Mismis's voice: "Does this mean the

65

Ice Calamity Witch is nearby?! Jhin and Nene, be careful. We don't know where the enemy could be hidiiiii— *Aaaaaaaaagggghhhhh*?!"

"Geez, I was just about to tell you not to run on the ice or you'll slip, but you managed to do it before I could even say anything…"

He could hear Jhin's exasperated tone, followed by footsteps.

But the entire surrounding forest was gripped by frost, meaning he couldn't tell their exact locations. Still, he knew his companions were close to reaching him.

The mages had figured that out, too.

"…Rin, we're retreating."

"B-but, Lady Alice?! Aren't we going to deal with him?!"

"We've destroyed the power generator. We know enemy reinforcements are coming—staying here would be dangerous."

The two witches dashed across the hill.

After using Rin's earth golem to gather the subordinate mages, they got back onto the monstrous bird they had originally been aboard.

"It was Iska, right?" The princess of the Nebulis Sovereignty turned around, blushing from the disgrace of her earlier blunder. She'd allowed him to see her face, even though she'd wanted to keep her identity a secret from the Empire. "I'll let you go for today. Don't think I'll do that next time!"

As the bird flapped its wings and echoed through the rustling trees, Iska watched the two girls disappear into the sky.

"Iskaaaaaa, I'm so glad you're safe!"

"Whoa, Captain?" He caught the childish captain as she leaped into his arms.

"I was so worried. Are you okay? Are you hurt?"

"…Why would you jump on someone when they could be hurt?"

On the other hand, Nene and Jhin were looking up at the hill before them and sighing.

"What's this? Hey, Jhin, is this really the work of astral power?"

"Just as the rumors say. It seems like she's no ordinary mage. It's like the Ice Age around here. There was even some snow at the rendezvous point on the front line."

"...It's exactly what it looks like." Iska glanced around the frozen forest and shrugged.

"How long has it been since you've been injured by an astral mage? Make sure you disinfect your injuries."

"Th-that's right, Iska. We need to treat them or they'll get infected."

"All right." Iska nodded, even as he felt his heart throb in his chest.

...Why is my heart beating so hard?

...I'm probably still wound up from all the fighting. But why? I've never felt like this before.

It might have been because of the lingering tension from the battle or because of something else—regardless, he failed to understand why it was happening.

CHAPTER 2

The Person I've Met

1

The united territory of the Heavenly Empire was known as the Empire for short. Its capital city, Yunmelngen, a metropolis that boasted the highest population in the world, was divided into three sectors.

Sector One was home to government affairs and research institutions, where those who carried the greatest authority gathered to discuss politics—including the Eight Great Apostles, who oversaw the Senate and made decisions on all matters regarding the Empire.

Sector Two was the residential zone. It was where 70 percent of the city's residents lived. The world's most prominent business district sprawled out next to it, attracting many tourists from the neutral cities to come visit every day.

Then there was Sector Three, the military base. Located here were manufacturing plants that fabricated the weapons designed in Sector One, along with facilities inside the extensive grounds to test them out, plus barracks for the Imperial soldiers.

"Sleeping here in this room is kind of nostalgic…"

Iska was at the very back of the first floor in Building 03, in what had been his personal room since the age of twelve. He'd been sprawled on the floor, looking up at the ceiling, since noon. He preferred sleeping on the hard floor over the soft bed, perhaps due to all the time he'd spent camping outdoors as a soldier.

"…And yet, I can't fall asleep at all."

He felt exhausted, but his mind was still raring to go, unlike his fatigued body. It had been two days since they'd been in the Nelka forest. He had only a brief time to rest until his next operation, but he knew he couldn't sleep.

"I'm an astral mage. Your Empire calls me the Ice Calamity Witch."

The reason for all this was the Ice Calamity Witch, Aliceliese. At least, that was the only reason he could think of.

Each one of her attacks had been on a scale that rivaled a natural disaster. She'd single-handedly overrun an Imperial base, and he understood why the Eight Great Apostles exercised such great caution when dealing with her.

"…Maybe that's why."

Ever since her mask had come off and exposed her face to him, he couldn't get the image out of his mind. She was an astral mage fit to be the Nebulis Sovereignty's trump card—with a charming, breathtaking beauty straight out of a fantasy. He guessed she was about the same age as him.

"Nope, no good. I need to think about something else!"

Any more daydreaming was going to dull his thoughts. He would be getting orders for his next task before long. In order to focus, he really needed to rest his body.

"Iska, are you here?" It came from the interphone.

That was when he heard a young voice coming from behind the door.

"Captain Mismis?" He opened the door.

Just as he expected, it was the petite, baby-faced captain.

"I was wondering what was going on with you, Iska... Look, you've been holed up in your room this whole time. You haven't come out at all, so Nene has been worried sick about you, too."

"I'm fine. I just haven't been able to sleep well."

"But, Iska, something's clearly been on your mind since we got back. I can see it on your face. You keep staring into space, looking at the wall." Mismis peered up at him with anxious eyes. "Um, ah, I... don't usually get a chance to act like a proper captain around you, so I thought I'd come to see if you need someone to listen to your troubles, 'cause you're my subordinate. Sometimes you just need to talk it out."

"You came all this way for that?" He glanced down at Mismis and noted that she was in her civilian clothes, which was unusual.

She was dressed casually in a shirt with a cute kitten appliqué and a childish three-tiered skirt with frills—probably because it was her day off.

But she had indeed come to visit him, even though she should be resting, too.

...There really is...no one like her.

Her skills as a soldier weren't great at all; her grades and exam scores had barely made the minimum cutoff. But the reason why Iska and the others wanted to work under Captain Mismis was for her empathy. She noticed the fluctuations of her subordinates' moods and reached out to them faster than anyone else.

She was charming in a way that made people want to follow her.

"See, I knew it. Iska, I thought you had a complicated expression on your face!"

"Do I?"

"Yeah, you totally do! Think of me as an older sister and tell me everything! Come on! But, well, I imagine it's about the events that transpired in the Nelka forest." The captain looked up at him intently. "Did something happen?"

"...I can't get that fight out of my head."

"You mean where you faced the Ice Calamity Witch? The battle ended in a draw, right?"

"...I was fighting for my life."

He still hadn't even figured out who was winning. It had become clear that neither of them could have stopped the other through sheer strength. They had been looking for openings in their opponent's moves. It felt like the psychological warfare of a first-class strategy board game, a battle of wits.

Whenever he'd caught himself thinking he had an advantage, he'd soon become anxious that it was a trap. Iska had never met an astral mage like that in all his previous experiences.

But—was that really the reason for his insomnia?

"Oh, and—"

"And?"

"...No. It's nothing." He pushed his partial sentence to the back of his throat.

The true identity of the Ice Calamity Witch is a really pretty girl. Those were the words he couldn't say.

...Anyway, that's not the reason why I can't sleep...I think.

...Plus, it would be embarrassing if Captain Mismis starts thinking I'm weird for saying that.

"Iska, I wonder if there's a scar on your heart."

"You mean a trauma?"

"Yeah. You endured intense combat, and now your heart has been hurt from fear and the pain of your wounds. It's not uncommon

among soldiers in the Imperial military. And you were facing that Ice Calamity Witch, so it wouldn't be that strange…"

It was the first time he'd ever encountered an opponent powerful enough to make him think he couldn't win. The battle might have planted that seed of fear in him.

Mismis's analysis was reasonable from an objective perspective.

But was that all there was to it? Was that really the reason? Iska was vexed by the feelings whirling in his chest. He couldn't grasp their true identities.

"Hmm. I wonder how we can address this. If the symptoms are bad, you would need to see a doctor." The petite captain crossed her arms, looking troubled. "In my case, I just eat barbecue and get a good night's rest when I'm anxious—then I feel right as rain. Wanna go get some grilled meat?"

"No, I'm not really in the mood…"

"Okay, that's fair. I do think you'll heal naturally with time, but it would be great if we could do something to get your mind off things for at least a little while… Oh, right! Iska, come here! Come here!" From her spot by his door, Mismis suddenly turned her back on him and started jogging. "I have something special for you, Iska. Come with me."

Building 01 of the Imperial barracks.

Iska opened his eyes wide in front of a door with a cute-looking rabbit sticker. "This is your room, right, Captain?"

"Yep, yep. My room's kind of messy, but come in."

In the living room, there were stuffed animals all over the warm-toned carpet, and on top of the table was a cup with a puppy print.

"Your animal collection has gotten bigger."

"Hee-hee-hee. What do you think? It's cute, right?"

"Yeah. Um…but that's kind of… I don't know how to put this…"

He was trying to talk about the thing that was hanging off the ceiling, where she'd been boldly letting her laundry dry smack-dab in the middle of the room. Iska tried to make his words as vague as possible, averting his eyes.

"I can't keep my eyes off that."

"What? What can't you—? *N-noooooooo!*"

She frantically waved her hands in front of Iska, desperately trying to cut off his line of vision. She'd forgotten her panties were drying in the room—the underwear of a lady in the prime of her youth.

"N-no, Iska! It's not what you think. I was just curious! All my friends have gotten themselves boyfriends, so I wanted to try something new, too. It's normal for a girl to want to test out a slightly more daring pair of undies sometimes. That's just how it is! Don't get the wrong idea!"

"I really don't get what you're trying to say."

"...*A-ahem.* Anyway." Mismis quickly squirreled away her underwear. "About our convo earlier. I feel like staying cooped up in your room won't do you any good. What you need to do is get yourself outside. That said, ta-daa!"

She held up a ticket that'd been on her table.

"Here, go to this and feel better."

"...The opera? It says *The Woman Knight Beatrix's Blighted Love.*"

"Yup, yup. It's performed every year in the neutral city. I really like it, so I bought ten tickets and saw it nine times, but I think I've had enough of it this year. That's why I'm giving this to you, Iska."

"What? But when am I supposed to—?"

"Do it before the next mission. Why not go tomorrow?" the captain proposed with confidence as she puffed with pride. "Oh,

it's wonderful. I'm sure it'll be a much-needed break. This is an order from your captain."

"…So it's an order now." Iska stared at the ticket in his hand and nodded.

━━━━━━━━━

White steam floated from the surface of the tub, which was filled to the brim with milky, hot water from the jowls of a lion-shaped basin filler. Flowers of all colors danced around various herbs in the water.

The giant bathtub could hold upwards of twenty people. Next to it, an ice bath was on standby, and a sauna full of piping hot steam was situated in the back of the room.

…*Plink.* The attendant approached on the wet tile.

"Lady Alice, are you still soaking in the tub?"

They were in the royal palace of the Nebulis Sovereignty.

The bathroom echoed with the sound of Rin's voice, and Alice opened her eyes as she lifted her face from the surface of the water.

"Why don't you come out? It's past your bedtime."

"…I'm not sleepy."

"The same as last evening, too. Normally, you would be too tired to even have your meal once you returned from the battlefield."

"It's just that I can't sleep."

The bath bubbled as she sank back into it.

Could it be because she'd gone to the Nelka forest? She'd mounted an assault with Rin and destroyed the power generator—just as her mother had ordered as the queen of Nebulis.

She'd executed the maneuver perfectly. There hadn't been a single mistake.

...So what in the world is this feeling?

...Why can't I get that swordsman off my mind?

She knew that was the reason behind her sleepless nights.

"Is it that soldier named Iska?" Rin stood barefoot at the edge of the bathtub in her usual housekeeping uniform. "You've been pondering over that swordsman's background since even before we got back to the Sovereignty."

"...I wonder who he is."

He was a boy about her age. Based on his appearance and mannerisms, he seemed young, but during battle, she could describe his movements only as fierce. He'd had piercing focus and an inhuman athleticism as he had dealt with Alice's attacks and cornered her. And while she'd experienced a fight against a formidable Saint Disciple in the past, that had been the first time she'd felt dread. There was no telling when his blade might have sliced through her neck.

"I am having others look into his past, but it may take several days at least."

"You've done more than enough. Thank you, Rin." She absentmindedly watched the flower petals floating on the water's surface as she nodded. "But that sword."

...There's no way. The sword just looks similar.

... I mean, my benefactor *wouldn't be in the Empire of all places.*

"That's right—it's just a coincidence."

"I'm sorry?"

"I-it's nothing!" Alice quickly waved her hand, flustered that Rin had heard her thoughts, which had snuck out of her mouth.

"Are you hurt? I can't believe an Imperial weapon would run wild in a neutral city..."

"But don't worry. I severed the wheel that maneuvers the frame. This thing won't be able to move anymore."

*　　*　　*

The memory was stained with the color of sand. She remembered sparks sputtering out intermittently and a dense cloud of dust.

There was the swordsman who'd helped Alice after she had been attacked, caught up in the commotion caused by an Imperial weapon. He was hidden under a veil of dust, and his voice was muddled, but she remembered the swords that glinted in his two hands.

One was black steel and the other white. These diametrically opposed blades looked exactly like the swords that swordsman had been holding.

"…"

In the bath, Alice put her hand to her ample chest, the sight of which made Rin jealously call her an early bloomer.

There, she could feel her heartbeat, pounding in a way that was puzzling even to her.

It beat faster: *Ba-dump, ba-dump, ba-dump.* Instead of settling down, it pounded with more force.

"Ugh, what's wrong with me? This is no good! I need a break!"

"Wait, Lady Alice, you're splashing water on me! Geez… please don't stand up so fast. You got my clothes wet."

"That's right—I need a break! Now that that's decided, Rin, let's prep for tomorrow!"

"…My clothes…" Rin pouted.

Alice gave her order, then quickly made her way to the dressing room, furnished with an entire wall that was just a mirror. She rushed over to the shelves and stretched her hand out to an accessory case.

"That's right. This is what I needed."

"Lady Alice, please don't walk on the floor without drying off. You'll slip and fall."

"I won't fall. I'm not a kid."

"And still you choose to run like one. Here. If you don't wipe yourself off, you'll catch a cold." Rin held a towel in her hands, holding it up to Alice's dripping golden hair as she tenderly started wiping away the moisture.

"Hey, Rin, look."

"*The Woman Knight Beatrix's Blighted Love*? ...Really? You made another reservation for the opera without telling me?"

After Rin finished taking care of the princess's head, she dried Alice's body, wiping the water dripping from the nape of Alice's neck to her back with the towel.

Rin had been born into a family that had been serving the royal family for generations. Though it was her duty to attend Alice, Rin was a year younger than Alice, making Rin one of the only close friends Alice could joke around with.

"It was such a pain getting this ticket. I had to apply to the lottery four times to get seats next to each other."

"...I understand. I'll accompany you." After she finished drying Alice, Rin dramatically sighed. "But are you sure you can do this? That swordsman saw your face very recently."

She meant the Imperial swordsman Iska and the recent incident when Alice's headdress had fallen off midbattle, letting him see her concealed face.

With her identity revealed, there was a fear that the Empire might dispatch an assassin. Alice had been momentarily nervous when the topic had come up before.

"It's fine. The more I think about it, the less of an issue it seems, really."

While the Empire regarded astral power as evil, Nebulis embraced it and far outpaced them in research. One thing they researched was the difference in astral powers among individuals.

There were multiple types of astral power dwelling in each person. However, Alice's astral power was even warier than most others, able to sniff out potential threats. When it sensed danger, it would automatically take defensive action. She had enough power to protect herself from a large-scale weapon of destruction, so she didn't feel the need to fret over one or two run-of-the-mill assassins.

"I'm not scared of the Empire's hit men. I have astral power, and if nothing else, I have you, Rin."

"…What a convenient time to praise me."

"It's the truth. Plus, I never wear my headdress whenever we go into a neutral city, right? Let's just go in our normal clothes." She fanned the tickets pinched between her fingers. "The curtain call is before noon, so we'll want to leave the royal palace before sunrise."

"Then I will prepare the sand bird. We must get going early in the morning, so please go back to your room, Lady Alice, and sleep. I will take the tickets for safekeeping."

"Hey! Rin, what are you doing?!"

"It's so that you don't lose them, Lady Alice. Moreover, please get some underwear on already. Or are you parading those around to show off?"

"I-I'm not showing off!"

Rin looked enviously at Alice's breasts, which seemed to bounce eagerly as they moved, and Alice turned her back to her in alarm.

"Please also inform the queen that you will be going out. You got into trouble for leaving without permission just the other day."

"…It's such a pain."

"Let me hear you say it."

"…Fiiiiiine." At her attendant's strict tone, Alice let out a small sigh.

2

Two years prior, on the day Iska was heading back home after receiving his unit assignment, he discovered that his master had up and disappeared.

More specifically, he boldly up and left right in front of Iska's eyes.

"The two of you—you and Jhin—were the only ones who didn't run away from me." For his parting words, his master imparted Iska with a touch of irony. "Well, I guess two is more than I expected."

This was the strongest Imperial swordsman, Crossweil Nes Lebeaxgate—also known as the Black Steel Gladiator. Back when he'd been the head Saint Disciple protecting the capital, he'd scouted boys and girls all over the Empire to find and train his successor—well, more like screen them.

Nearly half the candidates dropped out after half a day of training, and by the end of the day, 90 percent of them were gone. Three days after that, their numbers halved again. That continued for a year, then three years, then five years, until the only ones remaining were Jhin and Iska.

"Iska, weren't you the last candidate I brought on board?"

"Yes."

"I'm going to be honest: Among all the candidates, you were the one who was the most…"

"Y-yes?!"

"…Hopeless."

"Geez, you don't have to be *that* honest!" The boy haggardly collapsed in front of his master.

But the ebony-haired man, cloaked in black from top to bottom, spoke without reservation. "I scouted those who had the most promise and went from there. Meaning the last candidate would obviously have to be the most hopeless."

"...Well, I guess, but—" The boy puffed out his cheeks, unsatisfied by his answer.

The master had just handed Iska his pair of swords and now looked down at them pointedly.

"But you could have phrased it differently." Iska sulked.

"You were the one most like me. That's why I didn't expect much from you."

"—"

That was a truth, and this was the first time Iska had heard it.

His master—usually expressionless and tight-lipped, a person who'd normally give him listless looks—had voiced his "true feelings."

"Don't let these astral swords out of your hands."

"Of course. They're mementos of my precious master... Hey, ouch!"

The master punched Iska. *Don't call them mementos. Who said you could just kill me off in your fantasies?* That's what he seemed to say.

And there was one last thing. "Those swords are the only hope for the *rebirth* of the world."

"...Huh?"

"The astral swords will serve you. Now that you've touched them, they're locked, meaning only you can wield their power. That's why I'm giving you this responsibility."

He'd been given the role of ending the century-long war between humans and witches.

The master had told him: *That's your mission—as the Successor of the Black Steel.*

The sun scorched the earth, casting down a harsh heat that toasted the yellow sand until it was cracked and dry—leaving the whole region a vast desert spotted by a few sparse weeds. Attempting to walk barefoot on the scalding ground would have caused burns, even if it was for less than a minute.

Those were the Vishada wastelands.

A single ATV raced down the expansive desert roadway at a reckless speed.

"Iska, wake up, wake up. We're almost at Ain."

"Huh? Already?"

Nene shook the sleepy passenger from her spot in the driver's seat, causing Iska to rub his eyes. He could recall events up until the point when they'd left the capital before sunrise, but the scene around him now was wholly unfamiliar.

"It's almost noon. We've already been on the road for nearly six hours, after all. You were sound asleep no matter how much I tried talking to you."

"Sorry..."

"No worries. It's been a while since I've seen your sleeping face," Nene crooned happily. "Plus, you said you couldn't really catch any z's ever since we got back from the Nelka forest anyway."

"Yeah... I was dreaming about my master. I was remembering the time when he worked Jhin and me to the bone—a distant memory or, I guess, a nightmare."

"You mean Mr. Cross?" Nene asked as she gripped the handles

tight. "That must really take you back. You haven't seen him in your dreams for a long time, right?"

"It must be because it's the first time I've used the astral swords in a while. He told me to take care of them, but I let the Eight Great Apostles confiscate them from me. I was so relieved when they gave them back."

He looked down at the pair of swords leaning upright against his seat.

The ATV was headed to a piece of land that belonged neither to the Empire nor the Nebulis Sovereignty.

On the world map, these wastelands were designated as a wildlife zone for animals to run rampant. There had even been reports of a gigantic dragon sighting in the past. The roadway was safe, but it wasn't a place where many would feel comfortable drifting off.

"Ughhh, what a failure. Why did I have to sign up for a shift right when you wanted to go out, Iska?" Nene released the steering wheel with an incredibly deep sigh.

"Jhin's busy helping out at a firearms workshop, and Captain Mismis is on a shopping trip, right?"

"Yeah, I guess, but I wanted to hang out with you at the neutral city, too, Iska," whined the girl with the ponytail, plopping her head down on Iska's lap.

Apparently not even bothering to keep her eyes on the road, she used her legs to maneuver the steering wheel as the car sped down the highway.

"Nene, you've got to look where you're going. I mean, driving with your feet is…"

"But it's been so long since I've seen you, Iska."

"Has it really been that long?" He looked over to Nene.

...I guess she seems more mature now?

...She's gotten taller, and I feel like her face looks a lot more feminine, too.

A year of puberty had done wonders for her.

While Iska had been imprisoned, the young girl had matured into a woman. He imagined that if she let her hair out of her ponytail, she might have looked even more ladylike.

"Ngh." Nene grunted to get up and shook her ponytail, unsatisfied. "Damn...we're already here. Maybe I should have driven slower."

They caught sight of Ain, a neutral city that'd developed out of an oasis in the vast desert, and reached the entrance, which was enclosed by a gigantic wall.

"Thanks, Nene. I'll get on a loop bus when I head home."

"Okay, gotcha. I'll see you later, Iska!"

"...Yeah. Now then, where was that theater?" Iska watched the ATV drive away in a cloud of dust, then turned to the city streets.

Neutral city was the generic name for places that refused to choose a side in the century-long conflict between the Empire and the Nebulis Sovereignty.

"A neutral city, huh? It's been a while. I wonder how many years it's been?"

He found the theater, magnificent and proud, on the main road lined with buildings of all shapes and sizes. There was an impressive and elegant concert hall carved out of wood. And next door, a comparatively new opera house, constructed with modern design elements.

"It's as packed as always."

The fine arts bloomed in this city, which had accepted all sorts of artists who loathed the war between the Empire and the Nebulis Sovereignty—painters, musicians, poets, sculptors. Here, they'd developed a melting pot of culture.

Most of all, the neutral city Ain was known as the place for opera.

He watched the scores of musicians performing on the streets as passing tourists listened.

"—Oh, shoot. It's already time for the show!" Iska scrambled along the main street with his ticket clenched in his hand. "It was the third building down, I think. Crap! It's gonna start soon!"

He stumbled to the modern white entrance of the opera house.

"Can I still come in? Oh, I just barely made it? Phew. Thank you!" He jogged through the quiet hallway and into the performance hall. "...Pardon me. Just me coming through."

Iska slowly opened the door and entered the hall. The performance was just about to begin. It was pitch-black in the theater. He relied on the faint emergency lights at his feet as he looked for his empty seat.

"A seat on the second floor in the very front row. Wow, leave it to Captain Mismis. She's particular even when it comes to choosing where to sit at the opera."

In the inky darkness, he couldn't really see the faces of the guests around him, but they were women in affluent-looking clothes or aristocrats who'd stealthily come to the show with their families from a certain city.

"*With that, please enjoy* The Woman Knight Beatrix's Blighted Love." The announcement echoed through the hall as the curtain rose.

In front of several hundred onlookers, the opera began.

"*Farewell, my Beatrix. I cannot live alongside you.*"

"*...Yes. Fare thee well, Azel. The next we meet, it will not be at a church as this evening but on the battlefield.*"

In the middle of the stage, the actress performed the lead role of the eponymous knight, and the orchestra passionately accompanied the tragic tale with their performance.

"…Ahhh. I get why Captain Mismis likes this so much," Iska murmured to himself among the enthralled audience.

The knight's way of life was elegant and charming, her tragedy infectious. At that point, the other guests around him had been taken in by Beatrix's sorrowful circumstances, empathizing with her cause. He could feel they were moved to tears and watching with bated breath.

Among them, Iska was feeling oddly disillusioned for some reason.

"Oh, Beatrix! I can't believe you'd fall in love with a knight from an enemy kingdom… You're choosing the road of a forbidden romance—unrequited, no matter your love for him. How could anything be more tragic than this? This is too much! Why would God allow this…this horrible fate…? *Sob!*"

Iska seemed to have been seated next to the weepiest girl out of all the guests in this theater. By the end of the story, she'd become overwhelmed with emotion, crying so hard that her handkerchief couldn't dry her tears—and Iska couldn't concentrate on the stage anymore.

"You idiot, Azel! What kind of man are you?!"

"*Shhh*, you're being too loud, Lady Alice. Everyone else is watching quietly."

"B-but…"

"Come on. What happened to my handkerchief? I gave you mine after you soaked through your own."

"…That one is sopping wet, too."

"You're crying way too much!"

The girl started to wipe her eyes with the back of her hand. The theater was too dark to see her face, but Iska deduced from the sound of her voice that she was probably a teen. That seemed to be the case of the person sitting next to her, too.

"Um, here you go."

"What?"

With a stifled voice, Iska had offered his handkerchief.

...I mean, aristocrats love it when guys give their handkerchiefs to mysterious damsels in distress. They eat that shit up.

...And it's not that weird. I think.

He couldn't bear to ignore someone in need, especially when they were right next to him. But this was also a pragmatic move. If she kept up her wailing, he wouldn't have been able to pay attention to the performance.

"I haven't used it; it's completely clean. Um, I thought you'd be in trouble at this rate."

"..."

She must have been reluctant to take a handkerchief from a stranger. But she desperately needed to stem her stream of tears somehow, so the girl hesitantly reached out her hand.

"Thank you so very much."

Hmm? That voice.

He felt like he recognized her voice from somewhere, but he couldn't quite place it, especially because the pitch was strained. He might have just been hearing things. He quickly came to that conclusion and decided to redirect his attention to the ending of the opera.

When the curtains closed, applause rippled across the hall and lingered for a while in the darkness.

"Ugh... *Sniffle*, poor Beatrix!"

"Lady Alice, look. It's over now. Please at least wipe away your tears before the lights come on."

"B-but..."

The girl pressed the handkerchief to her eyes as she stood up, then bowed her head to Iska, who was still sitting in the next seat.

"Uh, um... I'm so sorry. I've made your handkerchief all soggy. Please let me reimburse you. Rin, please make arrangements to present the highest quality velvet available to him."

"What?! N-no, it's fine! That handkerchief was super-cheap."

"No, it's not a matter of price. You gave it to me when I was in such an embarrassing state." With the handkerchief gripped in both hands, the girl shook her head earnestly.

"Um, please let me thank you again," she muttered sincerely.

She took a step forward.

In that moment, the theater lights came on.

"Thank you for the handker..."

The glittering lights of the chandelier exposed her bright golden hair and sweet face.

It was the Ice Calamity Witch, Aliceliese.

The girl wringing the handkerchief in front of his eyes was the very same person he'd faced in an all-out battle a scant three days before in the Nelka forest.

"...Huh?"

"Wh...? Wh-wh-wh-wh-wh-what are you doing here?!" The princess of the Nebulis Sovereignty jerked her skirt away from him.

Instead of the royal garb cloaking her during their battle, she had come to the show in an unremarkable, plain dress. It could have been found at any clothing store in any city. She was the spitting image of a noble daughter secretly sneaking out.

"I see. You tailed me. Fine, then let's settle this right— Mggghhh?!"

"Lady Alice, you can't! This is a neutral city!" The attendant, Rin, had pinned Alice from behind. "Any and all conflict is forbidden in this city. It doesn't matter who you are. That is the law here. You could run into the murderer of your parents or an officer from an enemy country, but if you lay a hand on them..."

—1. Any conflict whatsoever is forbidden in the neutral cities.

—2. In accordance with the aforementioned clause, the first to act will be considered the transgressor.

—3. Embrace all culture and enjoy the fine arts.

Those were the common rules in every neutral city.

"...I know. I know I'll become an enemy to all those cities for breaking the rules if I lay a hand on him here. It would be a serious issue."

Alice brushed aside Rin's hands and bit her lip.

"But I can't believe I've been watching this opera next to you. That must be why I couldn't settle down."

"Uh, it seemed like you were way too invested in the show. I mean, with your bawling and all."

"—Ngh?! I—I was just sweating out of my eyes! Forget what you saw today, you hear me?!" Alice's footsteps rang out as she backed away.

"Lady Alice, you'll gather too much attention if you speak that loudly."

"Ugh, enough already!"

When the girl with flaxen hair finally realized the eyes of the other guests were on her, her face flushed even more than it already was from all the crying—making it blotchy and puffy.

"I'll be taking my leave now. Farewell, Iska!"

"...S-sure. The same to you?"

She gathered up both ends of her skirt, bowing courteously.

"Lady Alice, what do you think you're doing?"

"Huh?! Uh... D-don't get the wrong idea, Rin! It's force of habit!" When Alice realized she'd accidentally given Iska a greeting fit for the royal palace, she turned red to the very tips of her ears and sprinted up and out of the hall.

He was left alone in the theater.

"Geez, I was more surprised by you than you were by me…"

He placed a hand to his chest where his heart hammered away and breathed out, long and hard.

3

"…I felt like my heart was going to stop."

"That should be my line. I was worried about what I'd do if you caused a scene."

They had rushed away from the hall and parted the gathered crowds to go outside, spilling into the main street.

Alice finally calmed her fluttering heart. "He's not following us, right?"

"He's not. That swordsman didn't take a single step as we left the hall. Come to think of it, we should have expected this to happen."

Especially in this neutral city, which wouldn't side with the Empire or the Nebulis Sovereignty. In exchange for freely entering and leaving the city regardless of nationality, they had to accept the possibility of running into someone they recognized.

"…Still, I can't believe he was in the seat next to us."

"He's already seen your face. It's not as though another soldier has recognized you. The possibility of running into friend or foe is unavoidable in this city."

"R-right! …Let's calm down and go eat." Alice closed her eyes to set aside her rambling thoughts, then walked briskly down the main street. "I'm sure there is a famous pasta place nearby. I researched it and everything!"

"You really love your pasta, Lady Alice."

"I would be fine eating nothing but that for a whole month."

"It's not a matter of whether you'd be fine with it or not. I won't allow such a thing."

"Don't be such a tyrant. Look, it's over here." Alice took Rin's hand and bounded to the north.

They passed through the town square and turned a corner into an alley, where they were greeted by the sign for the pasta restaurant.

"I'm very sorry, but we're right in the middle of the lunch rush." A waitress in an apron bowed her head apologetically at the two of them. "I can seat you immediately if you made a reservation or if you're willing to share a table…"

"I don't mind. Come on, Rin, over here."

The pair sat side by side at a four-person table.

"Let me pour you some water, Lady Alice."

"Thanks, Rin. I was just feeling thirsty."

Alice was parched. Her throat was completely dry from bawling her eyes out at the show. When Rin passed her a glass, she immediately brought its rim to her lips, just as the waitress brought the other person to the table.

"*Mr. Iska, thank you for making a reservation.* Please make your way here."

"*Bwehhhh?!*" She spat everything out.

For the first time in her life, Alice spewed water from her mouth like a squirt gun.

"Whoa?!" The boy backed away from the table, startled. "What're you trying to do?"

"That's what I want to sa— *Cough…* Urg, w-went down the wrong way… Ugh… Wh-why are you here of all places?!" Alice

put her hand to her mouth. Her eyes welled with tears, but she glared at the young Imperial swordsman nonetheless.

"You brute! Not once but twice! So you really are following Lady Alice!"

Of course, Rin couldn't stay silent this time. She stood up from her seat and put her hand to the dagger hidden under her skirt.

…If I pull out my dagger, I'd be breaking a taboo in a neutral city.

…Wait. The prohibition on violence is worded as "the first to act will be considered the transgressor."

If that Empire swordsman attacked them first, Alice and Rin could lawfully claim self-defense, meaning they would be allowed to launch a counterattack without reservations.

"Um, I think there's been a misunderstanding."

"Don't play dumb. No doubts. No skepticism. I know exactly what you're trying to do."

Iska raised both of his hands to show he had no ill will.

Rin jabbed a finger at him. "When we parted ways at that opera hall, you were going off someplace else. Why are you here at this restaurant? If you have an excuse, then speak now!"

"This is the closest eatery to the theater. Plus, it's famous. I'm also the one who reserved this seat in the first place. You guys came after that, right?" Iska replied frankly.

"…" Rin froze in place. "…What do you think, Lady Alice?"

"He made a good point. But you can't let your guard down, Rin. We can't be careless."

"Geez, I can't help but overhear if you just talk in front of me like that. Anyway, I'm unarmed, as you can see. They kept my swords at the checkpoint by the gate."

With his arms still raised high, Iska twirled in front of them to drive home his statement.

They couldn't see anything that resembled a weapon. It seemed he was doing his very best to prove that he didn't intend to fight them.

"...Fine. I'll believe you for now."

The boy pulled out the chair across from where Alice and Rin sat.

"Lady Alice, are you sure about this? We may be in a neutral city, but we're still sharing a table with an Imperial soldier."

"Withdrawing here will make it look like I'm afraid."

If rumor spread of the Ice Calamity Witch fleeing the scene, it would give the Imperial soldiers more ammunition against her, and she wouldn't be able to face her own subordinates in the Nebulis Sovereignty.

"A-anyway, let's eat...," Alice muttered as she reached for the menu on the table.

Iska's fingertips brushed against hers as he tried to read it at the same time.

"Eep! S-sorry!"

"...Uh, n-no, it's my fault... Sorry." Iska shrank back as he withdrew his hand. "......Go ahead."

"......You should go first. I'll let you have it. You reached for it, didn't you?"

"......Yeah, to hand it to you."

"......Th-that's what I was doing!"

They ended up making a compromise: They left the menu in the middle of the table, where Alice and Iska looked at it from the sides, sitting across from each other.

...*The only problem is that our faces are too close.*

...*I mean, what am I thinking? We're just looking at a menu.*

She couldn't help averting her eyes from him. It wasn't as

though she didn't have male relatives, but none in the royal palace was close in age to her. She wasn't used to this situation.

"Um."

Alice reflexively went into high alert when someone suddenly spoke to her. "Wh-what is it?"

"Have you decided what you want?"

It wouldn't have been strange if the young Imperial soldier had declared, *I'll tear you from limb to limb right here and now,* but instead he was looking at her with mild-mannered eyes, talking to her rather demurely.

"…Right. I guess I'm ready."

"Yes! Be right there!" A seasoned waitress ran through the restaurant toward them. "And what can I get for you?"

""*I'll have a plate of your salmon and zucchini pasta with fresh cream sauce. Please make it* ben cotto, *or well-done, and keep the portion on the small side. After the meal, I'll take a cup of black tea with one sugar cube,*"" Alice and Iska recited together.

They'd asked for the exact same order, harmonizing with each other as if a beautiful melody.

"…Huh?"

"…What?"

Did I just say that out loud? They'd so perfectly been in sync that for a moment, Alice doubted who had even spoken.

And sure enough, Iska had the same confused expression.

"You're like two peas in a pod. Did you come here together?" asked the waitress.

""*No!*"" Once again, their responses overlapped perfectly.

"Lady Alice, compose yourself."

"You don't have to tell me, Rin. I know. Just for today. That's it. It's really only a coincidence of a coincidence of a coincidence!"

Alice inhaled as deeply as she could without the boy noticing.

...It's fine. I'm calm.

...We've got the same taste in shows and food, but that doesn't mean anything.

They collectively suffered through the awkward silence until their food came.

"Whatever. The food's here. Let's eat while it's hot." Alice twirled her pasta with her fork—then she stopped and snapped her face up.

A small spark of curiosity flitted through her head. She had something she wanted to confirm about this enemy soldier, especially since they'd continued to coincidentally align with each other.

"Do you like pasta?"

"...Are you talking to me?" His reaction was delayed. He hadn't expected her to ask him anything.

"Who else would I be speaking to?"

"Yeah, I like it. Well, it might be my favorite food. I love it with a cream sauce, but I think it's good even when you flavor it with nothing more than salt and pepper, too."

"Oh. You get it. It's so simple but so delicious."

Whenever Alice would ask Rin that question, her attendant's answer was always the same: "Please don't be picky and just eat." When she talked to the retainers at the royal palace, the best response was, "That's nice."

For the first time in her life, she felt something about the reply from her enemy: She was *having fun*. When she spoke to Iska, she felt her heart leap in excitement.

"But when the weather is this hot, I can go for a plate of cold pasta salad," she countered.

"Yeah, that's good, too. If they have sweet tomatoes at the market, I've just got to make it."

"Right? Cold pasta with tomatoes is so delicious. I like it, too! I could eat it every day when it's hot in the summer—"

"Lady Alice, you've stopped eating."

".......Oh," Alice whispered when Rin cleared her throat to admonish her.

The boy was not only a soldier from the enemy country, but he'd also seen her face. On top of that, he was a skilled fighter who could have matched a Saint Disciple in battle.

She'd forgotten all about that.

"I-I'm sorry. I've interrupted your meal..."

"S-same..."

They bobbed their heads at each other, bowing before returning to their quiet lunch. But as soon as they thought that, the young attendant let out a muffled whisper after she quickly finished her meal.

"It's common sense to cook pasta al dente, you amateurs."

""Ben cotto *is definitely the right way!*"" Alice and Iska spoke at the same time again, as Rin let out a sigh in resignation.

4

The stars on the black dome overhead glimmered with innumerable constellations, as if it were an overturned jewelry box. High above, shooting stars seemed to stream toward the horizon line. Alice had no doubt in her mind that the view of the night sky from the royal palace was the most beautiful sight in the world.

But she turned her eyes away on that night.

"Keep the events of this day buried deep inside you, Lady Alice."

"..."

Alice listened to Rin's words as she lay facedown on her bed.

"Normally, we would need to report this to the queen. I mean, we came across a soldier from an enemy nation, after all, even if we weren't engaged in battle."

"I thought you were the one who said we couldn't fight in the neutral city, Rin."

"I never thought we would sit down with him for a meal after our encounter at the opera house."

They were in the royal palace in Alice's room, which was called "Sion, the Jewelry Box of Bells."

Rin stood along the wall as she spoke to Alice in an unusually emotionless voice. "Luckily, we didn't let any secrets of the Sovereignty slip during our conversation today. If I wasn't confident about that point, I would have needed to inform the queen—no matter the circumstances."

"…I understand that."

That boy was a loyal dog of the hated Empire, the people who'd persecuted her ancestors and condemned them as witches and sorcerers. Iska was one of those feared beings. But why couldn't she shake off this unsettling feeling?

"Oh, this." Alice looked at the plain handkerchief next to her pillow.

He'd said it was a cheap thing that could be bought anywhere.

"I missed my chance to give it back…"

She'd borrowed this handkerchief at the theater. But she couldn't just give it back after she'd used it to dry her tears. That said, she hadn't known what to do with it regardless and brought it home.

"It belongs to a soldier of an enemy country. It shouldn't be a problem even if you toss it away."

"…But."

"That's why I asked for you to please forget what happened today. The swordsman, this Iska, is an enemy. He's not just your enemy, Lady Alice, but the enemy of tens of thousands of people who are just like you."

Rin turned her skirt up. By the time Alice realized that, Rin was already gripping the dagger that she used for self-defense.

It was quick, instantaneous.

On top of that, she'd also fished out a delicate metal needle as thin as thread, some steel string, and even a small set of explosives. Under her housekeeping uniform, Rin had hidden countless secret weapons, some of which even Alice didn't recognize.

She was a master at martial arts—a genius. That was one of Rin's many faces.

"Oh, the sage at the training tower was so disappointed that his student had become nothing but an attendant. I mean, you've mastered all his techniques—from the way of the sword, spear, archery, even torture. He said you had the talent to become a martial artist for the Sovereignty."

"He had a bad habit of letting his mouth run when he was drunk, too. Plus, I can't envision a single case where I would win in a fight against that swordsman Iska—whether by sword or physical combat or even if I used my astral power to its limits."

"Really, Rin?"

"That's right. I even think the sage would have been in peril during that battle."

Shrnk. The two daggers had made a high-pitched noise as they returned to their sheaths.

"I believe you understand this the most, Lady Alice, out of all of us. You revealed your *ice flower*—which you hid from the Saint Disciples—in a fight against a single soldier... That swordsman is

a monster. When you eventually challenge the Empire, he might be your greatest obstacle." Rin seemed frustrated.

But it wasn't unwarranted. Rin had found an opponent she couldn't stand a chance against, even as Alice's personal guard. She was resentful of her own uselessness when it came to this situation.

"That's why you need to forget about today, even if there's something you have in mind. That swordsman is possibly the most concerning threat to the Sovereignty."

Heeding Rin's advice was probably for the best. Even in Alice's eyes, Iska's power had been extraordinary. On top of that, he was still in his teens: If he continued to gain experience and training over time, she couldn't even imagine what a terrifying opponent he would become in the future.

…But the vibe he gave off today…

…It didn't feel like a bloodcurdling terror at all.

Rin had insisted it was only natural that he wasn't eager to fight her, since they were in a neutral city. But Alice had a different perspective of things. She thought he hadn't held any feelings of hostility at all; he hadn't been holding back or covering up a secret desire to get her. He really didn't have any intent to engage in combat at all.

…Plus, my astral power didn't react to him.

…And it usually tells me when my subordinates dislike me in the slightest.

Her astral power hadn't even remotely seen him as a foe.

More importantly, she'd let down her guard momentarily after they'd seen the show together and shared a meal. That was actually the biggest problem of all, now that she'd become aware of it.

She couldn't remain emotionless about it, leading her to hesitate over whether or not she should throw away his handkerchief.

"…But I think you're slightly to blame for this, too, Rin."

"Meaning?"

"Back there, you said making pasta al dente is common sense, and I ended up sympathizing with Iska, and it was super-weird."

"I was only speaking the truth. Pasta is best 'al dente. I won't accept any differing opinions."

"You're so stupid!" Alice threw the pillow in her hands at her attendant in the distance and curled up under her terry-cloth blanket.

———————

Sector Three of the Imperial Capital. Building 03 on the first floor.

In one of the rooms, Iska was lying flat on the ground and staring up at the light on the ceiling.

"…I can't sleep."

His eyelids were heavy, but even as he waited with his eyes closed for hours and hours, his consciousness wouldn't subside in the slightest.

Was it nerves? Or excitement?

…Neither.

…It must be because I saw that.

He'd seen Alice's breadth of emotions—from going to see the exact same opera to enjoying a meal together with an Imperial citizen—even though she was the one feared by the entire Empire as the Ice Calamity Witch.

"Lies, lies, lies." His lips murmured no louder than a zephyr. "The whole thing about her being a monster who doesn't bleed or cry? All lies. I mean, look at how much she cried. Even mages are just normal people."

He recalled her bare face.

Oh, if only those who feared mages in the Empire could watch

her bawl her eyes out. How many would seriously call her the Ice Calamity Witch then? Especially when she was such a dainty, delicate girl?

He might have been from the Empire and Alice from the Nebulis Sovereignty, but they weren't different at all. They were both human...

"...Ugh, why can't I fall sleep?"
"...Ugh, why is it so difficult to sleep?"

They spoke at the same time: A boy and a girl grumbled to themselves in the Empire and the Nebulis Sovereignty—two countries that were far, far apart.

CHAPTER 3

Binding Fates

1

Glittering in a vivid blue color, it was frozen over.

For the life of him, Iska couldn't recall *where* in the world he'd been in this memory. It was when the strongest swordsman in the Empire, the Black Steel Gladiator Crossweil, had brought him along all over the continent, journeying from city to city.

"The Empire isn't the whole world. Pay close attention."

"It might take you a decade or two to realize this, but you need this experience."

Under a certain set of circumstances, Iska and his master had separated partway through their travels. Iska'd headed toward the distant lights of a neutral city, crossing the plains at night. As he rode on a train, a group of wandering beasts had assaulted it for trying to sneak past their territory.

The small sword that he carried for self-defense had snapped

in two during the ensuing commotion, placing him in a bind. That was when someone had saved Iska's life—and it had been a witch.

A vivid-blue ice wall had shielded Iska, while pebbles of hail had knocked away the beasts.

...Did a witch just save me?

...Even though I'm from the Empire?

She was an ice witch. He couldn't make out her face, which was hidden in the dark veil of night, but he'd guessed she was a passenger on the same train.

The witch couldn't have known that this boy was from the Empire, seeing as they were so far removed from the Imperial capital. Plus, she'd also been attacked by the beasts, so defeating them was defending herself. She must have just ended up protecting Iska, too.

Regardless of her reasons, it didn't change the fact that he had been *saved* by her.

...But the Empire taught me that witches are cruel monsters.

...And yet, she saved me and the others around us, right?

That was the beginning of it. This event marked the moment that Iska started to rethink his perception of witches.

Maybe witches—or rather, astral mages—weren't bad people. If they could somehow talk to each other, they might have been able to come to an understanding.

Though Iska was of the Empire, he still believed in his intuition, even at present.

Imperial capital. Sector Three. Training area.

Waves of murderous heat beat down from overhead, and a blistering gale pushed the limits of 122 degrees Fahrenheit.

They were in the desert field. Just as the name implied, it was a training ground established for simulating combat in barren lands.

The tiny fragments of metals mixed into the gritty sand absorbed the heat of the sun at a higher rate, meaning the facility wouldn't drop in temperature lower than one hundred degrees, even in the dead of winter.

"Huagh… Haaah… Ah ahhhg… W-water…!"

A group of four shot through the outer rim of the field. Mismis was running caboose with a grim expression, as if it was the end of the world.

"Waaaaaaateeeeeer!" she shrieked in desperation.

"Geez, just drink some. I mean, the purpose of this exercise is to travel by foot *with* a supply of water." Jhin turned around as he darted over the sand.

The two of them were carrying backpacks with hydration devices, equipped with a straw for them to drink from while on the move.

"This activity lets us drink in exchange for carrying all this equipment on our backs. You've got tons of water on your back."

"It's all gone already. Jhin, please, water—please let me just have a sip!"

"You'll get bloated."

"Jhin, you're a big meeeeeanie!" Even though she claimed to be dead-tired, she seemed to have enough energy to screech back at him. "There's something wrong with this training area, I swear! We're being boiled alive by the sun while we run and get blasted by hot air coming from a ventilator behind us… Like, come on, we aren't laundry!"

"They're both great thermal weapons. I've seen them before." Nene pointed at a giant ventilator positioned to the rear. "We're able to train in the first place because we can re-create a desert. The researchers in Sector One can gather data from human experimentation and make even better weapons. What a great deal!"

"Nene, I'm scared that your mind would even go there!" The

captain squealed upon hearing the term *human experimentation.* "Uh, ahhh... L-look, Iska... Over there... I can see an oasis... There's an angel beckoning me ov...er...?"

"Whoa, Captain, wait! You can't go there! I think!" Iska shouted, trying to get Mismis to stop going into the light. He coaxed her into making the final stretch to the water supply station.

"I did iiiiit! M-my first victory on the desert field!" She dumped the backpack and jumped up and down.

"Wow, Captain. Just a little while ago, we would have needed to call for a stretcher for you halfway through."

"I know, right? I've been working as hard as I can to build up my stamina this past year!" Mismis pumped her fist, even as she was gushing with sweat from her forehead and neck like a waterfall.

From the looks of it, she was so happy that her fatigue had been blasted away.

...That's really something.

...Man, Captain, after all's said and done, you've really worked so hard while we were gone.

Iska swiped away the beads of sweat clinging to the ends of his hair as he took a stealthy glance at Mismis behind him.

Her baby face and petite frame made her seem no older than thirteen or fourteen. On occasion, her childlike looks caused ordinary soldiers to underestimate her, but Mismis continued working hard without becoming discouraged. Her tenacity had revealed itself in this training exercise, too.

"Ugh! Hey, Iska, you're ogling Captain Mismis." Nene puffed her cheeks. "Do you like that kind of stuff, too?"

"...That kind of stuff?"

"Sexy women."

Mismis had taken off her jacket, revealing a more casual outfit. Her arms stretched out of her white tank top, flushed red from

exertion. Slick with sweat, her clothes were taut around her body, hugging her curves and emphasizing her seductive waistline and her chest. As she sat drenched in sweat, her voluptuous form was more than enough to suggest that she was an *adult*—in sharp contrast to her childlike features.

"...I'm jealous. She might be short, but she's developed in all the right places." Nene frowned as she gazed at the captain enviously.

"Huh? Nene, what's wrong?"

"Ummm. Iska was looking at you funny, Captain... Mm-*guh*?"

"I wasn't looking at anything!"

He covered Nene's mouth in a hurry, using all the strength he could muster to shake his head vigorously from side to side.

"It's a misunderstanding, Nene."

"...Really?"

"Really. I just—"

The heat ventilator had been roaring in the background, pumping out a scorching gale capable of cooking a raw egg sunny-side up. But before Iska could finish his sentence, the wind changed to let out the nice, cool breeze of an air conditioner.

"...Whoa. It's cool. It's like a fan." Mismis tilted her head in puzzlement. "Did the machine break?"

"Come on—there's no way. We set it to the air-conditioning mode just for you, Mismis."

"Ahhh?!" The captain shrieked from the bench as a woman placed a hand on her shoulder from behind. "O-oh, it's you, Risya."

"Yoo-hoo! Isk, Nens, Jhin-Jhin, it's been a whole year. Do ya remember me?" Risya saluted them in jest.

Her face was shapely and seemed wise, pairing well with the black-rimmed glasses of an intellectual. Coupled with her height, she made a normal battle uniform look quite good. Iska was quite familiar with this woman of extraordinary beauty.

"How could I forget? It's not like there's a single soldier alive who would fail to recognize an active Saint Disciple."

"Isk, we were colleagues right up until a year ago, right?" She winked over the lenses of her glasses.

Her name was Risya In Empire.

To summarize her in one phrase, she was the unparalleled genius-of-all-trades—the Empire's pride and joy. Regardless of the field, she'd displayed prodigal aptitude and graduated at the top of her class at the military academy, mastering everything from academics, martial arts, gunmanship, and survival skills to strategic command. After easily clearing the rigorous combat exam, she had risen through the ranks from captain to Saint Disciple in no time.

"If I remember correctly, you're currently...the special guest at our defense headquarters. That's quite a feat."

"C'mon, it's no big deal. I mean, Isk, you were a Saint Disciple, too, just a year ago." *Ha-ha-ha.* She responded lightly.

Someone started speaking behind her.

"Iska might have been the youngest one to be promoted, but he was still at the bottom of the barrel in terms of Saint Disciples. In contrast, you're the adviser in the fifth seat and practically the right-hand woman to the throne. You're on a completely different level, even among the Disciples." Jhin stood up with an annoyed expression after he'd cooled down in the shade of a tree. "And? What kind of mess are you trying to push on us this time?"

"Just a small favor. Which brings me to you, Mismis." Risya stuck out her tongue jokingly before pointing a finger at the captain. "For your next mission, your unit is going to be working for me. I've already gotten approval, so I'm counting on you!"

"Wha...?"

"Hmm, are you unhappy?"

"'Cause, like, you're too smart, Risya. I'm not sure I'll be able to follow along with your strategy."

"It's fiiine. It's you and me, Mismis."

Mismis frowned as she peered up at Risya, who stroked the head of her former classmate.

"I'll have a handmade tactics pamphlet prepared just for you, Mismis. Just promise you won't lose it, okay?"

"Really?! Okay, I'm in!"

"All right! Jhin-Jhin, I'm counting on you to make it."

"You're forcing *me* to make it?"

"I didn't say *I'd* make it. Anyway, I came by to say hi. I mean, everyone in the unit—sans captain—is accomplished, right?"

"...Risya?" Mismis pouted.

"Ha-ha-ha, that was a joke. Yup, just a joke. You're great, too, Mismis. Plus, you know it's got to be true when I'm the one saying it!" Risya gave her another pat on the head.

Did they act this way because they were classmates and friends? It was unusual to see a Saint Disciple interact so intimately with a captain. After all, the former reported directly to the throne, and the latter was in charge of commanding only a single unit.

Those were their positions based on the strict doctrine of meritocracy.

For a young captain like Mismis, a Saint Disciple was supposed to be a target she would eventually conquer. To the Saint Disciples, the rank of captain was called the rank she'd long since conquered.

...I can't believe Miss Risya and Captain Mismis get along.

...I guess it's because the captain just doesn't have it in her personality to care about competition or bringing others down.

He remembered a time when Risya had met up with the captain in the past. Back then, the two of them had gotten excited

chatting up a storm about shopping even when it had nothing to do with mission planning.

That might also have been a testament to Risya's self-confidence. She could take up an easygoing attitude because she had unwavering conviction in her own genius and power.

"All things considered, you're moving things along too fast." With some discontent, Jhin turned a defiant smile on the officer—someone who was leagues higher than his own standing.

"We were dispatched on a military campaign to the Nelka forest just seventeen hours after Iska's release. That's the only mission we've done in a year. But you're making the snap judgment that you want us under your command. *If I were you, I'd give us more time.*"

"Meaning you want me to evaluate your strength a little more? Hmm, well, I'm planning to do that, of course, but I've basically sized you up already, ya know." Behind her glasses, the Saint Disciple's eyes squeezed into the shape of crescent moons. "You did a great job writing up the battle report on the Nelka forest. Accurate and concise. Not a single error or omission. You wrote it up, right, Jhin-Jhin?"

"Of course."

"When I read that, I could tell none of your instincts have dulled, and that applies to all of you." Leaving them with a wink, Risya flipped around to face Iska. "So then, Isk, how about we have a little interview."

"An interview?"

"What's your physical condition like? I heard from Mis that you haven't been able to sleep since the expedition into the Nelka forest."

"…I guess, sort of."

As a soldier, reporting on his physical readiness was part of his duties. It wasn't strange that a Saint Disciple would want to check

111

in upon hearing the news from Mismis. The only problem was that Iska himself didn't know why he couldn't catch some sleep.

The Ice Calamity Witch Alice. For some reason, her face would cross his mind, and then he wouldn't be able to rest easy at night.

"Sounds like you're not in tip-top shape. I heard from Mis that you went to the opera the day before yesterday. Am I correct to guess that hasn't really lifted your spirits?"

"Yeah, but it was fun. Um, it was nice to be in a neutral city for the first time in a while." He nodded enthusiastically.

...This doesn't seem like a good time to be honest.

...I shouldn't bring up the fact that I ran into Alice there.

"Oh, right. Thank you so much, Captain Mismis. That opera was great."

"I know, right? Oh, a tragic love story really hits the spot sometimes. It makes my chest seize up, but it leaves me feeling so satisfied." Mismis happily put a hand to her own chest. "Risya says they're no fun, though."

"I'm the kind of person who simply doesn't grasp high culture. Speaking of which, Isk, you've always appreciated music and art, right?"

"Yes. Um, have I mentioned my interests to you before?"

"My hobby is gathering intel. I love gossiping and hearing rumors about my underlings." Risya slipped her fingers into her breast pocket. "Isk, what comes to mind when I say Vribran Saril?"

"He was an Imperial court painter, I think. It's been...uh, about one hundred and fifty years since his time, so he was an oil painter before the hundred-year war."

"Bingo. Wouldn't expect any less from you. Well, I guess you can take this off my hands." The officer mischievously smiled as she pulled out a small ticket. "Apparently, they've got an exhibition going on."

"...Of Vribran's paintings? Is it in the neutral city?"

"Right-o. I won this thing by gambling with my underlings, but I feel like Vribran would be happier if you went in my place."

"But I just took a vacation yesterday..."

"It's fine. I'll have you make up for all the time you took off in labor. You're gonna play an important part in my next plan."

Risya continued to run her fingers through Mismis's hair. At least that's what the others thought she would do, but it seemed that she'd had enough, and she turned around.

"In conclusion, Mismis's unit is now happily under my command. We'll start by assembling next week. Then in a month, we'll begin joint training sessions. You're welcome to train up until then, or, Jhin-Jhin and Nens, you can take days off, too."

"And what about me? Can I take a break, too?"

"You're a captain, Mismis. No way, no how. We'll be having tactical meetings together."

"You big meanie!" Mismis pouted childishly as Risya happily poked fun at her.

Iska gave the two a sidelong glance. "...Guess I'm going back to Ain."

His reunion with Alice just two days before flashed through his mind. Of course, it wasn't like he'd serendipitously run into her again.

This time, he would be going to a solo exhibition of the *Imperial* painter Vribran. Plus, several days had passed since the incident in question. On top of everything else, there wasn't a reason for her to return to their last place of contact.

...Oh, I guess Alice ended up keeping my handkerchief in the end.

...Wait, why am I even thinking about this?

As if to clear away his errant thoughts, he gave his head a good shake.

2

The royal palace of Nebulis.

The estate was located deep within the Sovereignty—the state founded by astral mages. It was divided into three precipitous towers, and one of them was always open to the public. The specific tower that was accessible to visitors changed from month to month. In other words, the general public had the opportunity to see the entire palace over time.

The royals and the people had established a long history of trust. There was nothing to hide. They were brethren in their fight against the Empire.

However, there was one part of the palace that was not for the eyes of the populace, an area that could not be entered by anyone without explicit permission from the queen herself.

"I'm sorry I'm late, Rin. Did you wait long?"

"No, I just arrived."

Alice jogged over to Rin, who was lit dimly by the flickering light of a candle.

"I don't know how many times I've been here, but this place gives me the creeps."

They were in an underground passageway of a natural limestone cave. The air was tepid and moist, and a wind of no apparent origin circulated through the cave, caressing and tousling the top of Alice's head. Each time, she couldn't help but feel a chill, as though she'd been cursed by something.

"...Rin, help meee."

"Lady Alice, please stop latching onto me in fear. You're not a kid anymore."

"B-but what'll we do if we see a ghost...?"

"We'll be fine. Your astral power is stronger than any ghosts. Plus…" Rin continued to walk next to Alice, speaking to her in a tone that questioned why Alice had even bothered bringing this up now. "The one who slumbers here isn't dead."

"…I know that." But she still latched onto Rin's hem and refused to let go.

They wordlessly stepped down the uneven slope and noticed a dim golden light shining ahead.

It was the golden altar.

In front of it, a red carpet was rolled out over the bare rock, and on top of the altar stone was a brass candelabra for seven candles, a scripture scrawled with old writing, and countless other sacred vessels—whose names Alice did not know.

"I'm sorry I'm late, Mother."

"You're right on time." A woman in a lavender royal gown turned around.

Illuminated by the candles, her shimmering hair was gold with a hint of brown. Her ruby eyes were both kind and stern, mixed with a noble haughtiness.

She was beautifully somber.

That was Mirabella Lou Nebulis IIX—Alice's mother and the current queen of Nebulis.

Anyway, it was unusual for the queen to call upon Alice without an audience present.

"Alice, I want to talk to you about the events that transpired several days ago. You said you fought against an Imperial swordsman—one who wasn't a Saint Disciple, although he seemed as powerful as one."

"Yes."

They were talking about Iska. Alice had given her report on him right after their battle in the Nelka forest.

Her mother, Mirabella, was an astral mage with experience in battle, as well. They shared a history of fighting against Saint Disciples, and she was knowledgeable of the structure of the Imperial military, meaning there was a chance she would have known Iska's true identity.

But even she couldn't conclusively determine who the swordsman was.

"...I see."

"Mother? Is something wrong?"

The queen turned to the back of the altar. "See for yourself, both of you."

"Is this...a warning from the Revered Founder herself?!" Rin's shriek echoed through the limestone cave. Looking up at a black stone pillar in front of her, the attendant backed away in fear.

It is the Founder Nebulis.

The naked body of the Grand Witch had been crucified on the black pillar.

She had her characteristic tanned copper skin and pearly, wavy locks. She'd not only been the founder of the Nebulis Sovereignty—a paradise for all astral mages—but also carried the ultimate astral power in her.

She looked like a young girl no older than thirteen or fourteen.

"One hundred years ago, our Revered Founder was said to have stood up against some tens of thousands of Imperial soldiers on her own. *She's still alive even now.*"

The current queen continued to say in a humbled voice, "The Revered Founder had a twin sister—Nebulis I. She was the one who started the bloodline of the royal family—you and me, Alice. And although the Empire feared the Grand Witch, they did not know the Revered Founder had a sister. That was why when

Nebulis I passed on, the Empire rejoiced: They had believed the Grand Witch had disappeared."

But the Grand Witch Nebulis lived.

This was a truth that few in the Nebulis Sovereignty knew—other than the royal family and Rin's family, who had served them for generations.

Known as Nebulis I thereafter, the younger sister had become the queen and given birth to her children. However, the older twin had gone a separate way: The Revered Founder Nebulis was host to the world's oldest astral power, capable of changing the flow of time itself. At that very moment, she continued to lie in wait, constantly seeking an opportunity to exact revenge on the Empire.

And Rin had raised her voice in alarm because—

"Lady Alice, the ties on the Revered Founder are unbinding!"

The girl's body had been suspended in the air by a series of chain fasteners fixed on her arms and legs. They were starting to come undone.

"And this change occurred, Alice, at the same time you fought with the Imperial swordsman in the Nelka forest."

"…What could it mean?"

"Astral power responds when it perceives its host human is in crisis. For example, it was said that when Imperial troops arrived in the Sovereignty in the past, the astral power in our country reacted all at once. The same thing is happening to the Revered Founder."

The queen approached the black monolith that stretched to the roof of the cave. The Founder was fixed in place ten yards up.

"It's as though it's an omen of her awakening. Wouldn't you agree?"

When they heard the queen's words, Alice and Rin looked at each other silently. Until that point, nothing had happened when

Alice had fought units of the Empire. Did that mean the Founder had reacted to her fight with Iska?

"We have yet to uncover what conditions caused the Revered Founder's astral power to react." The queen shook her head. "It's said that one set of astral energy can resonate with other sets. Perhaps your powers are so strong that you've had an influence on the Revered Founder—at least, that's what the researchers at the Institute of Astral Power have hypothesized."

"It's true that was the first time Lady Alice exhibited that much strength," Rin offered.

While she listened to their conversation, Alice looked up at the Founder.

…You react to my power?

…There's no way that could have happened. Because—

That was because Alice had secretly gone to a deserted arena, far from the Sovereignty, to experiment with the limits of her astral power many times in the past. There had been multiple occasions where she'd released the same amount of power as in the battle with Iska.

And the Founder apparently never reacted to those times.

In other words, she'd basically never reacted before the fight against him. That was the only possible conclusion.

"…Iska. Just what are you?"

"Did you say something, Alice?"

"N-no! I didn't say anything!"

It seemed that the queen was taking the battle with Iska seriously.

…Then I can't ever say anything.

…I can't tell her that I saw him again the day before at that neutral city.

On top of all that, he'd seen her wailing as she watched the

opera, *and* they'd eaten together at the same table. It must have been a trick of fate.

...I need to forget about that. I'm going to forget it.

Then why did his face come back to her mind whenever she thought that?

"Regardless"—Nebulis IIX folded her arms together under her chest—"there are many unknown things about her astral power. We'll have the institute hasten their research, so, Alice, please refrain from fighting on the front—at least until we know more about the Imperial swordsman."

"All right. And on that note, I'll be leaving."

Let's go, Rin, Alice said with her eyes and turned her back to the Founder Nebulis, the Grand Witch, affixed to the black stone pillar modeled after a monolithic sword. It looked exactly like a black steel sword thrust into the ground.

"Awaken."

"The white astral sword can release whatever the black astral sword intercepted."

"......Did he say *'awaken'*?" Alice suddenly spun around on her heel.

The black pillar looked exactly like a sword in the ground. The fact that the pillar's color bore a striking resemblance to Iska's sword had to be a coincidence.

But the slumbering mage had stirred when Iska had said "Awaken"—when he'd released his attack with the white sword.

If she took her mother's words as the truth, that meant the Founder's astral power had reacted at the same exact moment as their battle. The ties that fettered her in place had started to come undone.

"Lady Alice, is something the matter?"

"...Uh! N-no."

I gotta stop. Alice cleared away her delusions. They were so unrealistic that she couldn't even call her idea a speculation.

For the time being, she would forget that she'd seen him again. He was the reason why she hadn't been able to get a proper night's rest. She didn't need her head buried in yet another problem.

"Oh, I think an art exhibition just opened the other day."

"Lady Alice, you couldn't possibly be thinking of going to the neutral city, right...?" Rin picked up Alice's mutter with her sharp ears and looked absolutely exasperated. "What happens if there's another incident...?"

"That was a coincidence. I'll make sure to avoid the opera. I didn't get a chance to really relax, so this time, I'm planning on taking my time and enjoying myself," she whispered, keeping her voice low to avoid her mother overhearing them.

They headed to the ground level, walking up the slope of the cave.

"Ain is having an exhibition of the impressionist painter Vribran right now."

"Vribran?"

"...Just talking to myself." If Alice mentioned he was an Imperial court painter, Rin would be sure to object.

Even though the Empire was an enemy, she couldn't deny that the arts and music had flourished there, having a huge influence on modern art. That was an unmistakable fact. In particular, the Imperial painter Vribran used color in the most nuanced ways.

Just looking at his work could soothe the heart. Ever since she'd seen a photo book of his pieces as a child, she'd wanted to see his real paintings with her own eyes.

"Rin, wait at the estate. The city's close enough, and I should be fine going alone."

Alice would have all the time in the world to relax and appreciate the paintings by herself until she was satisfied. She could feel her heart springing and dancing in her chest as she put the holy grounds and the slumbering Founder behind her.

"Yes. I'm sure it'll make any lingering doubts in my mind disappear."

3

The next day.

"Like! I! Said! *What are you doing here?!*"

They were in the town square of the neutral city Ain.

Alice had just pointed at the boy who'd coincidentally crossed her path. She yelled as loudly as she could.

"Iska?!"

"...Alice?! Why are you here?!"

He froze in place, too. And as if that wasn't enough, he held a ticket to the same exhibit for Vribran as Alice.

"How could w-we want to go to...the exact same exhibitions?! Why are you, an Imperial soldier, sauntering off to a neutral city so incredibly often? Don't you have a mission to protect the Empire or something?!"

"Okay, say what you want. But Vribran is an *Imperial* impressionist painter. It's not weird for me to see the exhibition. Are you even allowed to look at an Imperial artist's work?"

"There are no borders when it comes to art."

"And I'm simply going because he's my favorite painter."

Humph. They both glared at each other.

They didn't even notice the lingering stares of those passing by them in the square.

"I can't believe you'd be here to see an Imperial artist's paintings."

"Wh-why can't I?! I like looking at Vribran's foggy evening streets and sunrises. I can't paint for my life, but I can still appreciate art. Is that so bad?!"

"Huh."

"...What?"

"I was just thinking you're like me." Iska looked at the ticket in his hand and pointed at the large road right off the square. "I think the art museum is on this road. Want to head over?"

"Sure... I mean, wait, we can't!"

If anyone found out that the princess of the Nebulis Sovereignty was accompanied by an Imperial swordsman, there was sure to be an uproar—neutral city or not.

...And the royal family of Nebulis isn't exactly a united front.

...If I cause a problem, it'll also cause issues for my mother, the queen.

The queen wasn't unfamiliar with conflict. Even within the royal family, it was normal for them to plot and scheme against one another: Threats and groundless rumors were commonplace. Alice couldn't even remember how often she herself had previously been the target of unjust scorn for offenses she had no memory of committing. And the kicker was that those rumors had originated from her younger and elder sisters.

...The truth is, I was having trouble figuring out where the art museum was.

...No. You can't. Show him you aren't someone who can be pushed around, Alice!

She didn't have Rin with her, either. If someone saw her alone with Iska, they could start an unfounded rumor that a princess and swordsman of conflicting nations were having a tryst.

"You can go using this main road. I... I-I'll use this one!" Alice pointed at a small road her eyes just happened to spot.

"You're taking that little path over there?"

"Th-that's right."

"I hate to tell you this, but that road definitely only leads into an alley from the looks of it. You're gonna get lost if you go that way."

"I won't. Just you watch!"

"Hey, wait, Alice—"

She turned her back on him before waiting for a reply, even as she heard him continue to call out something behind her. But Alice marched forward and followed a small road—which veered ninety degrees off the main road that Iska had pointed out at the beginning of their conversation.

She strode down the path for a good few minutes.

"...Where am I...?"

Alice was in the mood to whimper out loud.

First things first, it was super-dark.

It was in the middle of the afternoon, when the sunlight should have been shining down on her relentlessly. But this little alley wasn't so much a path as it was a narrow gap between buildings, which blocked off the light and made it seem as dark as night.

"Plus, why the heck is it so gross? There's trash everywhere, which is really unsanitary and smelly..."

Something was encrusted on the wall, undoubtedly ghastly. It looked like a faded bloodstain, maybe traces of a drunken fight.

"Unbelievable. If I were a princess of this city, I'd order every single citizen to clean the whole place up... I mean, I get that it's a creative hub, but that doesn't mean people should only keep the main streets clean to maintain appearances."

She stumbled through the alley without a clue as to where she

was at the moment, relying exclusively on her intuition to head to the art museum.

Several more minutes later, Alice came to a sudden realization.

"...Rin, please help me."

She was hopelessly lost.

Alice had tried her best to skirt away from the paths stewed in raw garbage and any particularly dark alleys, which could only mean one thing: She couldn't even figure out the way back to the spot where she'd run into Iska.

"I even asked for directions to the museum partway..."

Maybe she'd phrased the question badly or they'd misheard her. Regardless, Alice wound up at a completely different town square.

"Wh-what's with this city...? At the very least, make navigating your streets easier on the tourists..."

Alice squatted down at an open bench facing away from a water fountain. She was far from finding the museum, and her legs were heavy from wandering through the filthy alleys.

By then, the sky was beginning to grow dark. A gray curtain began to close on the horizon far ahead, and the other tourists gathered at the square were gradually returning to their lodgings.

"..."

The mist from the fountain scattered the light of sunset and glittered with an amber glow. Through the screen of water, Alice could see two kids were holding hands and running around happily.

"...It's not like I'm lonely," she muttered in a raspy voice. "Once I get back to the palace, I'll have Rin. It's totally fine if I spend a day alone every once in a while..."

"Alice?"

She heard a familiar voice approaching her from behind the bench.

"I knew it was you, Alice."

"Huh? Uhhh, who could you...? Wait, Iska?!" Alice leaped up and yelled upon seeing him.

She hadn't been expecting him at all—making her heart pound painfully against her chest in surprise.

"Why are you here? What happened to the museum?"

"I already saw the exhibition. But I didn't see you there, so I thought that you really might have gotten lost. Especially 'cause, like, you chose to go down some random alley in the complete opposite direction of the museum."

"Ack..."

When he put it so bluntly, she didn't have any room to argue.

"Want me to take you there?"

"Huh?"

"It's already late. The visiting hours at the museum are going to end soon, so we gotta hurry," Iska suggested smoothly.

"B-but we can't. We're supposed to be enemies! I'm the princess of the Nebulis Sovereignty, and you're a swordsman from the Empire!"

"Oh, you're a princess?"

"Ah..." Alice froze in place when he pointed out that she'd revealed her own secret identity.

In their previous interactions, she'd told him she had a right to succeed the throne, sans details. Now he knew that the Ice Calamity Witch was the daughter of Queen Nebulis IIX.

"Well, I already expected as much anyway."

"...See! I knew there was no reason to hide that from you." Alice had a wide-brimmed hat pulled low over her eyes, which she took off, exposing her face to the sunset. "We're enemies. We can't go to the museum together."

"We're enemies, but..." Iska looked serious as he cocked his

head to the side. "You're the one who said there are no borders to art, Alice."

"…" She was silent despite herself.

Leave all conflict at the door and enjoy culture: That was the philosophy of the neutral cities.

Besides, Alice had come to see paintings by an Imperial painter. There wouldn't be anything strange about her *coincidentally* running into tourists from the Empire.

"…Yes. I did say that." She put the hat back on her head, but instead of pulling it down, she let it perch lightly on her locks of hair. "Please show me the way."

"In that case, follow me."

She chased after Iska. *Ahhh, I have to walk again…*

But Iska came to a halt as soon as she thought that—whether he could tell how she was feeling or not.

"We're here," he announced.

"Um, is it possible…?"

He pointed to the museum sign for the exhibition on Vribran. Alice looked at it and back to the town square immediately behind it.

"Was I lost right behind the museum?"

"Yup. The only reason I ran into you was because you were right there. Anyway, let's get a move on. We only have half an hour before it closes." Iska looked up at the wall clock beside the entrance. "I think it might be hard to see it all. Is there anything in particular you want to see, Alice?"

"Uh, um…uhhh… In that case, I'd like to see *The City in the Colors of Twilight*. It's a landscape painting of a city right before the sun sets in the winter from the perspective of a tall church rooftop!"

"In that case, it's over here." Iska quickly dived into the throngs going in and out of the building.

The tourists streamed past them. They went against the flow of people heading toward the exit and walked farther into the back of the building.

"This one, right? This is the one you wanted to see." Iska stopped and turned around.

Just past him was a painting that she'd swept her eyes over and over in her small photo book as a child.

It was the original, several times larger than the one in the book.

"...Oh..."

Her throat choked as her voice tried to rush forward, but she couldn't form it into words. What came pouring out wasn't the manifestation of thought but something born of emotion.

"...This is what I wanted to see." Alice took one step and then another toward the gigantic canvas that was as tall as she was.

A winter city blanketed in snow. The painting depicted the veil of night coming down on it. The colors weren't vibrant in the slightest, and the muted gray tones were chilly even to onlookers. But warm light flooded out of the windows of the houses into the night.

It was cold but warm.

When she was young, this curious scene had fascinated her. She'd been taught that the Imperial cityscape was a place that was filled with loathsome enemies, but she couldn't help feeling that the sight of it had the power to make her rage ebb away.

"Iska."

"What is it?"

"Why do you like this painter?"

"—This part." They were the same height, and he'd been looking up at the canvas next to her. With that, he pointed to somewhere around the middle. "The paint is thicker here."

"What about that?"

"This may be all a part of my imagination, but I like to think he rethought his next stroke just as he laid some paint down with his palette knife. It's like the moment he tried to put the scene in his head onto the canvas, he thought of something even better. So then he stopped and thought about it."

"...I see."

"And right there. He blotted out the original color with a completely different one. I feel like the scene in his head was constantly changing as he painted—more intense colors, more passion."

In the midst of his explanation, the footsteps of the patrons heading to the exit echoed throughout the gallery, but Alice had ears only for the boy standing beside her.

"I think you know this, too, Alice, but the painter Vribran would only paint landscapes of places like city streets and roads or harbors. There was never a single person in any of them. His subjects would always be inanimate and his colors dark, but—"

"It was still incredibly passionate?"

"Right. I feel like he must have been a quiet person on the outside, suppressing intense feelings on the inside. His paintings show you his true personality, and I think that's why I like them so much."

"I completely get that. I also—" Alice started to speak, but the princess of the Nebulis Sovereignty suddenly realized something.

She realized that she'd been enthralled—not by the painting but by the profile of the boy standing next to her.

*　　*　　*

She'd been taught the foundations of art by painters in the Sovereignty, but none of them had understood how Alice had felt. It was because Vribran was a painter from the Empire. The painters of Nebulis thought themselves to be better. That was all they were occupied by.

This was the first time someone had humored her and tried so hard to put to words their impressions about her favorite painter.

"Alice, what's wrong?"

"…It's nothing," Alice answered quietly.

She needed to feign composure. Otherwise, she had a suspicion that a part of her would become unrecognizable.

━━━━━━━━

It was sunset.

They were the last guests at the museum, lingering until it closed. Alice and Iska left the exhibitions together, heading to the square behind the museum.

When they got to the bench where she'd gotten lost earlier, Alice tossed him a glass bottle glistening with droplets.

"…Here. To thank you for showing me the way. You must be thirsty after talking so much."

"You really didn't need to." Iska caught the bottle of fruit juice in the air.

Alice turned to him and held up her own drink. "I don't want to be indebted, especially to you."

"It wasn't a big deal or anything. I have the money to… Huh?" Iska dug through his pockets and froze.

"What's wrong?"

"...I might have forgotten my wallet."

"You forgot to bring money?"

"Well, um... I was preoccupied trying to not forget the museum ticket..."

"Then how did you get here from the Empire?"

"I had a pack of tickets for the loop bus."

"Meaning you forgot it because you didn't need to use any money."

Yeah. The boy seemed apologetic as he slumped down. He looked back and forth between the bottle of juice in his hand and Alice's face before opening his mouth in a hurry. "Oh, but I can definitely pay you back..."

"You silly goose." The faintest of smiles broke out over her face.

This was the first time Alice had let herself smile naturally at an Imperial soldier, even if it was a small one.

"I just said I was giving it to *you*. Don't worry about it."

The water fountain lit up under the sunset. They were too embarrassed to sit next to each other on a bench and chose to rest by the water's edge a short distance apart.

"...Come to think of it..." Alice held the now empty bottle in her hands as she turned her eyes to him. "How old are you?"

" I'm sixteen. Seventeen this year."

"...Oh? Then that means I'm a year older than you."

They were nearly the same age. She'd had a hunch that was the case, but she'd never imagined he was the younger one.

"So you're younger, huh. You could speak a little more politely to your senior, you know."

"I don't wanna hear it from a senior who was lost not too long ago."

"Y-you've got that all wrong! I was merely sightseeing around the city!"

Their conversation veered off to other trivial topics: They talked about painters other than Vribran and a bit more about pasta again. And then they reached an unexpected lull without either of them intending to stop talking—because they'd dozed off.

When Alice realized that she'd fallen asleep for a moment, she saw that the sun was on the verge of sinking into the horizon.

"Uh, wh-what am I...?!"

She hadn't been able to fall asleep for an inexplicable reason for days, and yet, she'd fallen asleep without a worry in front of an Imperial swordsman. It was a foolish act. She looked reflexively to her side.

"...Iska?"

He was sitting on the edge of the fountain and nodding off, his head bobbing as though he was on a boat. His eyes were still closed, and she could hear him breathing softly in his sleep.

"Are you asleep?"

He was probably pretending. Alice tried moving away to check, causing him to shift.

"..." The boy let out a gentle snore and fell right over on her.

He buried his face in her chest.

"Aaah?!" Without thinking, she froze up all over. "Wh-what do you think you're doing?!"

"..."

"...Seriously, how are you sleeping so comfortably? You're such a kid... I mean, well, I guess I was nodding off a bit, too."

But he was a little too defenseless.

She started to think that maybe he hadn't been able to sleep for a long time, either, as she listened to his gentle breaths.

"Aren't we supposed to be enemies? I know we're in a neutral city, but do you really think you can let your guard down? I...I... If I wanted to, I could finish you off in one blow..."

No response.

She glanced down on his peaceful expression for a moment then tilted her face toward sky and sighed deeply. "If you sleep in a place like this, you'll catch a cold, silly."

She carefully held Iska in her arms as he leaned toward her and laid him down. She checked that he was still asleep.

"Excuse me." Alice stopped a taxi driving by the road. "Please take him to the Empire, up to the capital's entrance."

"Come on." The driver didn't even try to hide his scowl behind the windowpane. "You can't be serious. At this hour? It'll take me six hours to get to Imperial territory, even if I step on it. Plus, the capital? I won't make it till late into the night or early tomorrow morning. How much do you think that'll cost? Add in the long distance and overtime, and it's gonna make it stupid expensive."

"I'll pay the fare up front."

"What? Up front? Do you even know how much—?"

"Please take this." Alice pulled out a round bundle of bills and tossed it toward the driver before he could launch into another tirade.

It was a stack of the common currency used in this world. It was enough to buy a new taxi outright and then some, much less cover the fare.

"And keep the change."

"...Thank you for your business."

"Make sure you take care of him."

"Yes, ma'am!" The driver dashed over to the fountain and hauled Iska onto his back before carrying him to the passenger seat. He gently laid Iska down. After he got into the driver's seat, he peeled away toward the city walls.

"Don't get the wrong idea. This is just to say thanks for taking me to the museum. That's all." Alice watched him leave until

she couldn't see the taxi anymore and then once again turned her back to the square.

Time to go home.

...But why would I fall asleep?

...I haven't drifted off on any other day except today.

After all, she'd been awake since the day of their battle in the forest, unable to get a wink of sleep because Iska's face had been burned into her mind.

According to Rin's theory, the tension from the battle hadn't completely dissipated yet. But if that was the case, there was no way she would have dozed off right next to Iska himself.

"Seriously! What's going on?!"

The haze over her brain was far from disappearing; in fact, she felt as though it had gotten even denser.

Alice punted a pebble on the road with all her might.

CHAPTER 4

Between the Mission and the Heart

1

Sector Three of the Imperial capital.

"Uhhhhhgh…"

They were on the second floor of the military base in the strategy room for platoons. In the completely enclosed, soundproofed room, a petite captain with blue hair groaned in front of the mountain of documents piled up on a table.

As Iska took a seat next to her, he handed her a bottle. "Captain Mismis, look! I bought you your favorite soda."

"Yay, you got me ginger ale!" Mismis's face lit up, and she snatched the dewy bottle as though she were a predator leaping on her prey.

"Nene and Jhin, I got some for you guys, too. Let's take a short break."

"That's unusual."

"What?"

"That it's bottled instead of in a can." In the seat across from

Iska, Jhin folded his arms, looking somewhat dubious. "Did they sell out of the ones in cans?"

"No. I guess I wasn't really thinking about it. I kind of just... went for these."

Iska hadn't noticed it until Jhin had pointed out that he'd brought them bottles glistening with droplets of moisture.

"To thank you for showing me the way. You must be thirsty after talking so much."

"...Come to think of it, it could be 'cause I got a bottle from her."

"Got? From whom?"

"Oh, no, no, no! Nope, nope. I meant that the person at the store handed them to me when I bought one. You know, when I went to the neutral city." Iska shook his head in a fluster as Jhin scowled and pressed him for details.

He couldn't say that he'd gotten a bottle of juice from the Ice Calamity Witch. Even if he did tell them, it would be sure to confuse them even more.

...Oh yeah, how did I get home?

...At some point, I wound up in a taxi, and before I knew it, I was back at the capital.

The driver had already been paid, too.

He hadn't immediately understood the situation when the driver told him. Even if he'd half-consciously stumbled into a taxi on his own, there was no way for him to have paid for the fare, since he'd forgotten his wallet, after all.

In that case, the one who'd covered it up front must have been...

"I can't do this anymore!" Mismis's chair clattered as she shot up from her seat. "Too many things to memorize! What *is* this? I

mean, we have to wait until next week to know more about Risya's mission for us! And we're gonna start training *next month*, right? Why do we have to study all this material beforehand...?"

There were documents piled nearly a yard high on the table.

And it wasn't just one stack. Behind that mound of papers, there were other piles of the same height, forming an entire mountain range.

"Arg. I can't believe I need to hammer this info into my head to guarantee our survival. It's just too much to handle."

"Oh, they totally said that there's no guarantee we'll make it out alive even if you memorize all of it."

"Nene, I really didn't need to hear that!" Mismis hunkered down in her seat once again.

But this time, she slumped forward and slammed her face onto her desk.

"When we get tired from hitting the books, we have to do strength training. When we get tired from training, we go back to studying the documents. If we get tired from studying, then we go train again... No one will tell us more about the mission, meaning there's no way to keep my anxiety in check."

"We can expect that the mission must be some seriously shady crap." Jhin was continuing to speed through the documents. "Come to think of it, Iska—"

"Yes, hellooo. Mismis, where are you?"

A broadcast cut Jhin off. They heard Risya's voice, likely originating from her strategy room in the central base.

"How's everything going? You haven't gotten on Jhin-Jhin's nerves by grumbling about how much material you need to memorize, right?"

"Eep..."

"And you definitely haven't asked Isk to go out and buy drinks for you, right? Bad girl. A superior can't boss around their subordinates

outside of our missions. That's against regulations. Oh, but if you've got an extra ginger ale, I'll take one, too."

"You're watching us! You're watching us, aren't you?! Hey, come out here!" The captain's eyes swept across the room, which shouldn't have had a surveillance camera.

"Anyhow, let's put that aside. Isk, could I ask you to go somewhere?"

"To over where you are?"

"Nooope. Try the Imperial Senate." The fifth seat of the Saint Disciples didn't even try to hide her sarcastic chuckle. *"I think you've forgotten by now, but you used to be a fugitive, ya know. Who do you think got you released?"*

"…I remember."

The Eight Great Apostles were the ones who commanded the greatest authority in the nation, standing at the top of the Imperial Senate and holding sway over the whole capital in place of the Lord.

"They've finished reading your report about heading to the Nelka forest. So yeah, that's why they've summoned you."

"…They couldn't be imprisoning Iska again now that they're done with him, right?"

"Well, don't get riled up, Nens. This is the first I've heard about this, too."

Nene looked at Iska anxiously.

In contrast, Risya's voice over the broadcast seemed carefree, mixed with a big old yawn. *"Anyway, head over. Be there by four in the afternoon at the usual place."*

"It must be some more seedy business." Jhin leaned back in his chair. "Those Eight Great Apostles never mean good news. Our master thought they were the biggest phonies. I wouldn't be surprised at whatever they've come up with this time."

"…Yeah."

The Black Steel Gladiator Crossweil had loathed them far more than he did the Nebulis Sovereignty or any astral mages.

Never trust the Eight Great Apostles.

They were said to be the most influential people in the Empire, tasked with the duty of protecting the Lord.

"Anyway, I'm heading out."

"Iska! I-if something happens, I'll come running right over as your captain!" Mismis's tone was more serious than ever.

He nodded in response to her protective, maternal expression and left the room behind.

———

The Imperial Senate, otherwise known as the "Unseen Will."

That nickname was based on the fact that the assembly hall was nowhere to be found on maps. Soldiers who needed to know the location were always verbally informed by their superiors. It was never communicated in written form.

Iska had learned where it was for the first time back when he'd been promoted to Saint Disciple.

"It's over three miles underneath the capital…"

This far down, the ambient temperature exceeded three hundred degrees.

The facility was located in the depths of the planet, where microbes could barely survive. The only way into the Unseen Will was through an industrial elevator at the central base.

…All this just to hide it from the Nebulis Sovereignty.

…They're so thorough.

Even if the astral mage corps decided to burn the whole Empire to the ground, the Eight Great Apostles wouldn't feel so

much as an itch. As soon as he stepped into the Senate hall, he felt like he could already hear the mocking laughter of the Eight Great Apostles.

"Sorry to keep you waiting."

Iska looked to the front of the room to the monitor set on the wall. It flickered with light, and eight figures indistinctly floated into view. They were the Eight Great Apostles, those with the Empire under their thumbs. Iska could see only the outlines of their forms on the monitor.

"Now then, Iska, the Successor of the Black Steel. We have read your report."

"You fought the Ice Calamity Witch, and she withdrew. Outstanding, as expected."

The Eight Great Apostles spoke in an exuberant tone. Iska was secretly relieved that they were in a good mood. He was already nervous about the fact that he had been summoned by his betters, but because he could never tell what these Apostles were thinking, the whole ordeal was even eerier.

"But I wasn't able to protect the power generator."

"Your mission was to stop the Ice Calamity Witch. It wasn't to protect the reactor."

"Now we know that the Empire has the power to face the Ice Calamity Witch. We praise you for confirming that for us. That was more than enough. We'll take that into consideration when we deliberate on possibly re-promoting you to Saint Disciple."

Saint Disciple—Iska's head snapped up when he heard that phrase come from one of the Eight Great Apostle's mouths.

That would be way too fast.

In the Empire, might was right. It was a meritocracy. He could think of some cases where a rank-and-file soldier with outstanding abilities would suddenly be promoted to captain… But even with

that in mind, he'd been imprisoned for committing treason. How could he be allowed to become a Saint Disciple again so quickly?

"We understand that you wish for peace. If you become a Saint Disciple, you may be granted an audience with the great Lord. But in order for you to be promoted, we need to pull the wool over the other Saint Disciple candidates' eyes. This is especially the case since you're an infamous convict within the Empire."

Iska heard a low chuckle come from the monitor—from a man in his prime—and he could also make out the voices of an elderly man and a young woman.

"We will offer you the conditions for your promotion. That is—"

"To capture the Ice Calamity Witch."

"Urg! But Alic—" He narrowly kept himself from spitting out her name.

Even he didn't know why he'd tried to hide it. But there was a part of him that didn't want to thoughtlessly hand over the name Aliceliese Lou Nebulis IX to the Eight Great Apostles.

Iska understood that he and she were enemies.

But could he really do it?

...To capture Alice with my own hands.

...And hand her over to military headquarters... That would be...

"How old are you?"

"...Oh? Then that means I'm a year older than you."

He recalled her faint, joking smile.

She'd let him see her heart thaw for the briefest of moments, even though she was an enemy. That memory surfaced unexpectedly in his mind, animating the scene with stunning vividness.

"There is no time limit for this mission. But make haste if there's anything in the Empire that you hold dear."

"Make haste? What do you mean?"

The Eight Great Apostles had spoken as though they foresaw a disturbing future and too momentously for it to be a threat to Iska alone.

"Have you heard the legend that *the Grand Witch Nebulis lives on*?"

"I heard it a few times as a kid."

It was like a spooky story, shared among many in the Empire. But the tale wasn't something to take seriously. People treated it the same way they would if someone spread an apocalyptic rumor that the world would end in a year.

"But what about that…?"

"Hmm, it seems you really have no idea."

He heard an amused laugh.

"The one who spread that legend in the Empire was none other than your master."

"My master?!"

"We seek the truth."

"*The Black Steel Gladiator Crossweil hid that from us.* We thought there was no logical reason that you wouldn't know as his successor, but we were off the mark… *In that case, we are done here.*"

"*Put this out of your mind.*"

They appeared to lose interest in this soldier. The Eight Great Apostles' tone started to frost over—to become cut-and-dried.

"You worry about capturing the Ice Calamity Witch. Succeed, and we'll promote you to Saint Disciple. Of course, if you make a mistake, we will have to imprison you, as per our previous agreement."

"We expect great things of you."

"Begone. We will inform you about the next operation through Risya In Empire. All you need to do is follow through."

"..."

Iska wordlessly gave them a slight bow.

Unable to say anything, he turned his back on the Eight Great Apostles.

═══════════

He was half-asleep and half-awake until nightfall.

His vision and thoughts blurred as though he'd been caught in a trance. He went back to the base where Captain Mismis, Jhin, and Nene were waiting; then the four of them fell into silence as they read through the documents outlining the mission. But he didn't manage to process a single piece of information.

In fact, he couldn't even remember returning to the barracks. When he came back to his senses, he found himself in his own room in a fetal position, lights still off. Iska was deep in thought as the night wore on.

"Why do you like this painter?"

Alice was an enemy—the daughter of the current Nebulis queen and the purebred descendant of the Grand Witch Nebulis, the one who'd led the revolt against the Empire. She was a menace to the Empire and was known as the Ice Calamity Witch.

Had he ever encountered any other enemy as powerful as her?

And had he ever seen a more fitting target for his attacks?

If he managed to capture her, the balance would tip in the favor of one country: With Alice as their shield, the Empire could

negotiate peace with the Sovereignty, and Nebulis wouldn't be able to reject them. The Eight Great Apostles were targeting Alice for that reason without a doubt.

But there was something on his mind.

"...Maybe they're not," Iska whispered as he looked out the window at the starlight cutting its way into his room. "Can't we get along without some peace conference or holding each other hostage?"

But if he didn't capture her, they wouldn't be able to hold peace talks at all. That had been his line of thinking up until that point. It was the reason he'd battled against the astral mage corps and sprinted around the battlefield trying to capture a purebred.

...But I was wrong.

...Alice was smiling, even without some peace conference.

Iska and Alice.

They couldn't exactly be called friends, but they'd passed the time together in the neutral city without conflict. Didn't that mean the Empire and the Nebulis Sovereignty could do the same?

Couldn't they get off their path of conflict without forcing a negotiation for peace?

"..."

Iska stretched one leg out and raised the other to his chest, cradling his knee with one hand as he used the other to pick up his communications device. Its light blinked. He waited patiently for the other end to pick up.

"H-hewwo...? I-Iska... It's the middle of the night... Mmmgh... What's up?"

"I'm sorry for contacting you this late, Captain."

Mismis sounded incredibly sleepy. He waited for her to become fully conscious.

"Okay, okay, Iska. I'm up now."

"Sorry for the sudden request, but please let me take the day off from training tomorrow."

"Huh? Wh-what's wrong?!" On the other line, the captain's voice ricocheted up an octave. *"Take a break? Are you feeling under the weather? Or are you feeling unsatisfied with my command? ...I–I'm sorry, Iska. I'm nothing but a failure as a captain......"*

"No, no, that's not it."

"Oh! It can't be... Is it because I sneaked out to get some barbecue for dinner tonight without telling you? Sorry, Iska, I didn't think you were craving it, too."

"Geez, no! That's not it!"

Ahem. He coughed. Even as Iska felt his hand tighten around the communicator, he squeezed out his request.

"I have something I need to do. In the nearby neutral city."

"The neutral city? What? But you were there just the other day to see paintings. Risya gave you that ticket, right? And you went before that with my opera ticket."

"I'm not going there to see anything. There's someone I want to see and talk to."

"And?"

"Well, I'm going to talk about something kinda complicated, so it might end up taking a while... Or we'll end up fighting and going our separate ways right after."

With that, he tried to let out a wry chuckle, but the only thing that spilled from his lips was a raspy voice, filled with self-derision.

"I plan on pushing off early in the morning. The place is far from the capital, so I think just the round trip will take about ten hours. I don't know when I'll get back."

"Which is why you need the day off."

"Yes."

The four of them were planning to train together on that day.

Without him, they would need to reschedule. He had no doubt that he was causing trouble for Captain Mismis, and for Jhin and Nene, too.

"Is it important?"

"...Yes. Please let me do this."

The captain was silent on the other end. After ten excruciating seconds, he heard a long sigh come from the other side.

"Oh, well. If you're that insistent, I suppose."

"Thank you so much."

"But on one condition: I'm going with you tomorrow."

"What?"

Why do you want to come? Iska faltered for a second, hesitating over whether he should ask her to clarify her intentions. A few beats of silence passed between them.

The first to speak again was Mismis.

"Look at yourself in the mirror."

"In the mirror?"

"Iska, you've got a tense look on your face right now, don't you?"

"...Uh." Iska half-unconsciously opened his eyes wide.

"See! I knew it. I heard you gulp just now." Mismis let out a giggle. *"I mean, your voice sounded strained from the start. And you called me this late at night. You were pretty caught up in your thoughts, weren't you?"*

"...I don't even know how to respond." He put his hand to his forehead and breathed deeply.

Most of the time, he couldn't say that his captain was quick on her feet by any stretch of the imagination or that she had a good memory. But she was scarily perceptive and could sense when her subordinates' moods had changed.

"You've got me. I shouldn't have expected any less from you, Captain."

"Heh–heh–heh. Yup, well, anyway. Like I said, I'm against you going by yourself. Even your tone of voice didn't sound normal or even remotely okay. I can't have a subordinate go somewhere alone in that kind of state."

"…I understand." He nodded.

He would need to file a report of the incident anyway, regardless of how it turned out. Besides, it would be easier to show *her* what his position was if Mismis was there with him as his superior.

"Captain Mismis, I'm counting on you."

"Whoo-hoo! All right! By the way, what should I wear? If we're going in civilian clothes, I'll need to be fast to pick out an outfit in time!"

"Your normal combat uniform will work just fine."

They were fighters from the Empire. That was how he planned to attend the meeting.

"Well, I'll see you at six in the morning tomorrow in front of the carport." Iska hung up the call.

As he continued to look at the night sky through the window, he realized he was feeling frighteningly sober.

2

"Lady Alice?"

In a passage overflowing with light, someone had called Alice's name as she was going back to her room from the community bath at the royal palace.

She turned around. "Rin, where were you? I wanted to take a bath with you."

"……"

"Rin?"

Her attendant was tight-lipped, silent. Her amber eyes pierced

through Alice in an expression that wasn't easily decipherable, like anger or anxiety might be. A different emotion colored her face—one of deep concern.

"I have something I need to speak with you about."

"What could that be?"

The attendant spoke in a stifled tone. "We have finished looking into that Imperial swordsman."

"You mean Iska?" She'd been wondering about his background for so long.

...I've run into him twice in the neutral city.

...But it's not as though I could ask him directly.

He would have been a match for the strongest of the Empire—the Saint Disciples.

But he was a private, not even a captain. On top of that, his ferocity melted away whenever he stepped off the battlefield. To Alice, he seemed gentle and like the type to let down his guard. He was a normal boy.

"Tell me."

"Yes. But, well, not in the hall."

"Of course—we'll do it in my room. Let's go."

They couldn't know who would cross their path in the palace halls. And in this case in particular, Alice and Rin had been keeping the fact that they'd seen Iska in the neutral city Ain a secret from the queen. If anyone overheard them, it would be an inconvenience to say the least.

"The investigation sure did take a while."

They were in Alice's room—Sion, the Jewelry Box of Bells. Alice made sure to close the door with her own hand.

"It's been a while since I asked you to do this for me. I thought a few days would be more than enough for you and our agents to

look into a mere foot soldier. I mean, it would be a different story if he were a Saint Disciple."

She hadn't thought she'd bump into him twice between then and now. By this point, she knew his favorite dish was pasta and that he appreciated opera and the arts.

Her agents would never be able to sniff out this intel, and she couldn't believe that she'd been able to gather so much information about him without much effort.

...Oh, and he has a cute face when he's asleep.

...Wait, what am I thinking?! I need to be taking this seriously right now!

"Let me hear it." Alice kept her internal discord at bay as she nodded to Rin. "...Who is he?"

"A Saint Disciple." The attendant did not mince her words. "It seems he was the youngest boy to ever be promoted. It's no doubt that he's distinguished even among the generations of Imperial swordsmen."

"A Saint Disciple?! Wait, Rin, that can't be right."

There was a total of eleven Saint Disciples in the Empire. Each and every one of them had the potential to deal catastrophic damage to the astral mages, which meant the Sovereignty had been pouring resources into gathering information about them for decades. Even Alice had hammered the eleven Saint Disciples into her head.

"How could I not know that Iska was a Saint Disciple...?"

"It's because we don't have any logs of him in our war records. After his promotion, he was immediately imprisoned and stripped of his rank, and he never stepped foot on a battlefield."

"Imprisoned?" Alice's eyebrows knit together.

Why would someone with enough talent to be a Saint Disciple go to jail?

"And the circumstances?"

"...I'm sorry, but I'm not sure what to say." Rin thrust a faded copy of an Imperial tabloid magazine at Alice with an uncharacteristically shaky expression.

"Iska, the Youngest Saint Disciple in History.
"Imprisoned for treason against the nation and aiding the escape of a witch. Given a life sentence."

...Life sentence.
...But wait, what is this thing about aiding the escape of a witch?

The magazine was dated a year ago.

"There was a 'witch'—meaning, astral mage—captured in Imperial territory, and he let her out of prison, which lead to him losing his status as a Saint Disciple. I tried consulting other sources to confirm its authenticity and came to the conclusion that the contents in the magazine aren't wrong."

"Which means he was immediately demoted afterward. That's why I didn't know about him."

"It's not just you, Lady Alice. The agents were just as surprised. However—"

Rin touched her hair parted in the middle of her head, tied on either side. It was a nervous habit of hers. Whenever she was deep in thought, she would end up unconsciously running her fingers through her hair.

"As you're aware, Lady Alice, he was acquitted."

"I know that well."

"He was released eleven days ago, a day before you fought that swordsman in the Nelka forest."

Iska had been released in order to fight the Ice Calamity Witch.

It made sense: He was strong enough for the Empire to come to the realization that he could challenge a purebred by himself.

"But the more I think about it, the less I understand it." Alice looked down at the page from the tabloid magazine in her hand. "Aside from our time together in the neutral city, I know Iska was seeking me out when I met him in that forest. If I remember correctly, Rin, he even asked *you* if you were the Ice Calamity Witch."

"Yes. Though I'd rather not recall my blunder..." Rin's tone turned gruff, as though she'd remembered the moment the tables had been turned on her offensive. "Anyway, you're right. That swordsman certainly had the intention of fighting against the Nebulis Sovereignty. It may be more accurate to say he had the goal of fighting the Ice Calamity Witch—of fighting you."

"In that case, why would he release one of our allies a year ago?" She couldn't help pointing out this inconsistency.

On the one hand, he'd let a witch escape imprisonment; on the other hand, he'd challenged Alice and Rin in order to capture them.

...But to the Empire, aren't we all just witches?

...What's the difference between the witch he helped and me?

"The prison break might be a trap in order to fool us."

"Rin, please look into the mage who received his assistance."

"I've already made the arrangements. It will take a few more days."

"You're quick. I expect nothing less." Alice nodded in satisfaction and perched on the corner of her bed.

That's it for today. I'm going to sleep now. Alice wordlessly gave her cue to Rin. It was a sign that they'd developed over the course of ten years—with Alice as the master and Rin as the servant. This was one of the many signals between them.

Another was when Alice shot a glance at the teacups in the

cupboard. That meant "teatime." And when Rin hiked up her apron, it meant "I must attend to other business and take my leave." They had an unspoken understanding of each other.

With that, Rin left the room. After Alice confirmed that the sound of her footsteps receded down the hallway into the distance, she reached under her pillow.

"No one's noticed, right...?"

The handkerchief. It was the one she'd borrowed from him in the neutral city of Ain. Alice had told Rin that she'd burned it a while back, when Rin had insisted that she would dispose of the enemy's possessions herself. In actuality, it had been hidden under her pillow the entire time.

"...I can get rid of it at any time." Alice knew it sounded like an excuse, but she couldn't go through with it just yet.

She still hadn't been able to ask Iska about his real intentions.

"You're the one who said there are no borders to art, Alice."

...I don't know.

She didn't know why he'd given her his handkerchief to wipe away her tears. She didn't know why he'd shown her the way to the museum or devoted himself to telling her about the paintings.

Maybe it was in order to deceive the enemy. Maybe Rin was right, and it was a trap. Maybe these innocent moments with him in the neutral city were all just an act.

She could wait until after that was confirmed before disposing of the handkerchief. It wasn't as though postponing it would make a difference.

"It seems you've become quite interested in an enemy soldier."

"Mother?"

The door had been opened without a knock, and her mother

was there in her daytime gown, even though it was late into the night. Alice guessed that she'd finished her official duties, and she was about to retire to her own room.

"Wh-what has brought you all this way?" Alice quickly hid Iska's handkerchief behind her back.

"I heard that you ordered Rin to look into that soldier. But I've already put my intelligence department in charge of handling it. Alice, you don't need to worry about it."

"..."

"Or is there a reason why this piqued your interest?"

"No, I merely overstepped my boundaries."

It seemed no one had seen her running into Iska at the neutral city. Alice finally came to this realization based on her mother's demeanor and secretly breathed a sigh of relief.

"It was a part of tracking the enemy's movements..."

"I can understand why you were trying to take this into your own hands. But extend them too far, and your sisters, Elletear and Sisbell, will glare at you with envy."

Elletear was Alice's older sister, and Sisbell was the third and youngest sister.

Both of them were first-rate astral mages, purebreds. In the Sovereignty, they were renowned as important and talented women involved in government affairs.

They were also her rivals to succeed the throne...

Elletear and Sisbell had eyes all over the royal palace. As the middle child, Alice could feel at home only when she was in her own room with Rin.

"And one more thing. It seems you're collecting paintings by Imperial artists again." The queen was referring to the bookshelf along the wall in her room.

With a look of exasperation, her mother glanced at the photo

books lined up on the very top of the shelf. They'd been painstakingly collected by Alice, since they weren't in general circulation in the Nebulis Sovereignty.

"The Empire is the enemy." Alice had heard her mother say this countless times before. "It's the den of those who detest and persecute us, the ones who call us witches and sorcerers. Don't forget that in the past, the Empire conducted witch hunts without mercy, and countless mages fell victim to their depravities. As a mage, it should be your lifelong desire to destroy the Empire and bring it to its knees."

"…"

"It's the same with the Imperial arts. You're aware of the Empire's paintings depicting 'witch hunts' and 'trials'. The artists are simply more Imperial minions. Collecting these photo books is completely absurd."

"…Yes, Mother."

"That is all I have to say. I've kept you up late enough."

Her mother left the room.

Alone once again, Alice stood still for a while.

…Is it really like my mother says?

…Are all the people in the Imperial territories unforgivable monsters, without exception?

"What are you?"

"You infiltrated our Imperial base alone and broke through our defenses. And you took out our power generator. You can't be a normal astral mage."

Iska was different.

Even when she had met him in the Nelka forest, he had never used the derogatory term *witch*. He'd carefully selected the words

astral mage, she remembered. On the flip side, her mother was asserting that the people of the Empire were indiscriminate savages who knew them only as witches and sorcerers.

Who is the one discriminating against whom...?

Alice brought the handkerchief from its hiding spot onto her lap, staring hard enough to bore a hole straight through it.

"Okay, I've decided!" With a long exhale, Alice flew out of her room, striding through the silent hallway.

"Rin! Hey, Rin! Are you awake?!" Alice burst into the room next door. "I need you to make preparations to go out."

"Wh-what's going on?!"

Rin spun around in her pajamas, gripping her nightcap in her hands. Her hair was straight down, and her pigtails were undone, making her look more mature than usual.

"We're leaving the royal palace first thing tomorrow. We're going to the neutral city. Make sure to prepare by then."

"Again?!" Rin's voice was close to a shriek. "But if we run into that swordsman Iska...!"

"We're going there to see him."

"...Pardon?"

"I want to check for myself. I want to know his true intentions." Alice bit her lower lip and turned her back on her attendant. "I'm sure this will be the last time."

3

The street was blazing hot with the sun at its peak, tracing a line overhead from its place on the horizon during the wee morning hours.

The coppery earth was parched, covered in cracks and fissures

that stretched out in the shape of a spiderweb. Tufts of weeds dotted the wasteland, which didn't have a drop of water to spare.

"The neutral city of Ain, huh. It's been a while since I've gone by car."

They were in an ATV zooming through the plains. Mismis was at the wheel, and she narrowed her eyes to counteract the blinding rays of sun.

"I told Jhin and Nene about this situation. They're gonna focus on personal training for today."

"Thank you."

"Yeah. Anyway, it's such a nice day out. Not a single cloud in the sky."

The wind rushed through the roofless vehicle, tousling the captain's hair as she stomped on the gas pedal in good spirits.

"So, Iska, I'd be so happy if you'd tell me who we're planning on meeting today."

"Who do you think it is, Captain?"

"An important person in the Empire. My guess is a Saint Disciple other than Risya. 'Cause, Iska, you were just summoned by the Eight Great Apostles, right? Are you planning on holding a secret meeting someplace outside the Empire?"

"I'm not that amazing."

They began to see glimpses of the neutral city of Ain across the horizon. Iska started to recall the streets of the city, famous for its opera and paintings, as he smiled wryly at the captain.

"I didn't know any of the Saint Disciples. Plus, I was demoted immediately."

"Rumor has it that those eleven are really competitive anyway... Hmm. But if that's the case, I don't know who in the world we're meeting up with."

"We're not meeting up."

"What does that mean?"

"I just had a feeling they would come. I've never believed in fate or destiny until now, but…but…I think I'll see her again."

"Meaning?"

"I won't know until I get there." Iska shrugged at Mismis, who looked ready to bury her head in her hands.

From the front window of the car, he stared off at the city.

"By the way, Captain, is there something in the sky?"

A soaring black shadow blotted out the clear blue sky. From their perspective, it looked like it was coming from the northeast—approaching the neutral city of Ain by following the path of the sun.

"…It's a bird. Captain, it's a huge bird."

It was a monstrous bird straight from the world of myths. With a body in the shape of a Steller's sea eagle, it had a tail that was long and waved in the wind like a snake. The white plumage had hints of blue, giving it a marbled effect.

It looked like a white cloud trailing through the blue sky, as though the colors of the backdrop had come to life.

And it was massive. They could clearly make it out with their naked eyes from the ground, meaning it would be far larger than a human if it landed.

"Oh, how rare! It's an albatross! It's a kind of living fossil!" Mismis let out a happy hoot from the driver's seat. "It's an ancestor to modern birds. They don't really nest in Imperial territory anymore. You know how we use a ton of guns in training exercises, right? They don't like the sound of gunfire, so they've all run far away."

"To outside the Empire?"

"Yup, yup. But albatrosses are sharp; they'll become your watchdog if you feed them. Train them enough and they'll let you fly on their backs. There are a few villages far from the Empire that

raise them. For example…" Mismis followed the path of the gigantic bird with her eyes. "…They say the Nebulis Sovereignty keeps several. I've seen reports about that."

"…Nebulis?" He kept his eyes peeled as he stared at the albatross, not wasting a second to blink.

The bird had flown in from the northeast. That was the direction where the Nebulis territories were sprawled out, just as Mismis had said.

It might have been an illusion, but he thought he could see something on the back of the albatross.

"…No way."

"Iska?"

"Captain, please drive up to the entrance. Stop the car there."

The albatross flew above the wall and descended toward the city. They followed it, heading to the outskirts of Ain in the ATV.

"Hey, hey, Iska! How are we gonna find the person you're looking for?"

"I think they just arrived, too." Iska looked to the sky, at the albatross, rising as though sucked in by the blinding sunlight.

It had finished its task of ferrying its master to the neutral city, which meant it was getting ready to return to its nest in the Nebulis Sovereignty.

"Over here."

"Uh, okay?"

Iska swept his eyes through the streets of Ain and signaled to the captain with his eyes as they entered the city blooming with the fine arts.

On the roads, the musicians didn't seem to mind the heat and lined the streets with their performances, just as Iska had seen before the opera show. Artists spread their canvases, and the tourists happily watched.

It was a peaceful moment. The concept of time could be forgotten altogether.

Outside this city, a war raged between the Empire and the Nebulis Sovereignty. But it was as if this scene was an attempt to demonstrate that people could live without conflict and war.

"—" Iska stopped in front of the square.

"It seems we're completely in sync. I wonder which stars we could have been born under," mused a beautiful girl holding a parasol aloft.

She wasn't in her civilian clothes, which she'd used to sneak out in private. At the moment, she was wearing the same brilliant royal gown as their first encounter.

"About that albatross from just now."

"We're raising it at home. When it was a chick, it was small enough to hop around on the palm of my hand, but it's grown so much in four short years. It can fly much faster than any Imperial car."

"Oh, Lady Alice. How can you say that? Just earlier, you were saying, 'Rin, faster, faster! It's a race! We have to get there faster than that car—no matter what!' You made such a big deal of it."

"Rin."

"…My tongue slipped." Rin retreated behind her.

After giving her attendant some side-eye, Alice closed her parasol in one graceful movement.

"Right. About the taxi from the other day—" Iska started.

"What could you possibly be talking about?" For the briefest of moments, an amused smile played over the princess's mouth.

But she immediately pursed her lips, and her eyes faintly narrowed, though she wasn't looking at Iska—but at the captain with blue hair next to him.

"By the way, who's that little girl?"

"She's my superior, Captain Mismis."

"...I see. That's how it is, huh?" Alice muttered and handed her parasol to Rin.

"Um, Iska? Who is this pretty girl?"

"She's—"

"It's fine. I'll introduce myself." Alice cut off Iska and placed her hand to her chest as she lowered her voice to prevent passersby from overhearing them. "Pleasure to meet you, Imperial Captain. I am Alice—Aliceliese Lou Nebulis IX."

"Miss Alice? Uh, but... N-Nebulis?"

"Oh, I wonder if I can clear things up by saying I'm the Ice Calamity Witch. That's what they call me in the Empire."

"—Erk?!" Mismis had a full-body spasm. "Uh, um? It's a joke... Right, Iska?"

"It's true."

"Wh-wh-wh-wh-what's going on?!"

"We have something to discuss." Alice's gaze was fixed on him until the very end. "Let's go outside. Come with me."

"Got it. Captain, let's go."

"...What's going on here?"

Iska dragged the dumbfounded captain along with him as they followed the pair ahead of them. Alice faced the front the whole time. Rin attended her, keeping pace beside her while occasionally turning to check on Iska and Mismis.

"We won't try to run. And there isn't anyone else from the Empire except the two of us."

"S-silence! I'm the attendant of Lady Alice. It isn't strange for me to be cautious around enemies. I mean, don't talk to me!" Rin faced forward again.

He watched as she reached a hand under her skirt reflexively.

He knew there had to be an arsenal of weapons hidden there for self-defense.

"How curious," murmured Alice.

As Alice led the way, her eye was drawn to the far right corner of the street, where an artist was facing a canvas and painting a family portrait.

"Why do we choose to hate each other when we could be living in this kind of blessed city?"

Alice wasn't talking to Iska or Mismis. Her murmur might have been directed at herself.

They took a step out of the city walls, facing heat from the sunlight and the burned hills spread out in front of them into the distance.

"It's hot."

"Lady Alice, your parasol."

"—But this is all I need." The Ice Calamity Witch snapped her fingers. "I can just freeze as much as I want."

A chilled wind erupted from the ground by her feet. In the blink of an eye, she'd cooled the scorching sand for several hundred yards ahead of them.

It was a carpet of ice.

"Wh-what is this…? Even our latest weapons wouldn't be able to change the temperature this much." Mismis took her next steps cautiously. "Y-you must really be the Ice Calamity Witch…"

"I think she's doing it on purpose," Iska commented.

She was making sure the captain knew who she was. Out of all possible courses of action, this performance was more than enough to persuade them.

"I guess this is far enough. No one will be able to hear us here. It seems that neither of us has anyone tailing behind." The princess stopped dead in her tracks.

They'd carefully made their way along the ice carpet for ten minutes, walking until the neutral city had become a vague outline in the distance. When they climbed a hill, Alice finally turned around.

"I know you know why we're here. You're the Imperial soldier who was caught for treason a little over a year ago. You're the weird Saint Disciple known for breaking a mage out of an Imperial prison."

"……"

"I looked into your background. You know about me, so it's only fair, right?" Alice looked down at him.

"I guess."

"Plus, there's no way you could only be a private. You're too strong of a swordsman. That is, unless that captain is stronger than you, in which case the story would be completely different."

"What? Th-th-there's no way that would be true!" Mismis hopped up in alarm as the Ice Calamity Witch glared at her. "More importantly…wh-what business do you have with us?! Why would one of the biggest VIPs be waiting for Iska? I don't get it!"

"There's something I want to ask him." Alice gave Rin a look.

The attendant took out a faded tabloid magazine. Iska had seen it before, a report shown to him countless times while he'd been behind bars.

"First, is this true?"

"There's no denying it."

"Were you imprisoned for a year for letting a mage get away?"

He nodded without a word.

"Why?" Alice demanded.

"…It was a young girl—twelve or thirteen. Her astral power was weak. But the Empire doesn't take that into account when it captures mages. And I couldn't stand it."

"There are some inconsistencies between your actions and

words." The Ice Calamity Witch's voice was thorny. "You were waiting for me at the Nelka forest so you could attack and capture me. Here you are trying to catch one mage, but you would have me believe you let one go in pity just over a year ago?"

"……"

"So you have nothing to say. What's wrong, Imperial soldier?" Rin barked. "Cat got your tongue now that Lady Alice has found your weak spot? But I remember you asked me whether I was the Ice Calamity Witch. You must have involved the imprisoned witch in some sick scheme—"

"I'm not contradicting myself." Iska cut her off.

Rin went silent in the middle of her sentence, as if she could feel the intensity of his emotions.

"My goals haven't changed. They're the same now as they were a year ago."

"What does that have to do with the article from the magazine?"

"Peace negotiations." That was all Iska said in front of Alice.

It was the first time.

It was the first time he'd revealed his vow to a Nebulis mage.

"I want to stop the war. But it's not as though the Lord will listen, and I don't think the Nebulis queen would, either."

"Obviously." Alice nodded and spoke with a cold tone. "Are you trying to say that you desire peace? That's impossible. How deep do you think our hate for each other is? Until one side surrenders, the war will never end."

"That's right. That's why I thought about catching a direct descendant from Nebulis's bloodline. I was going to capture one of the strong mages who are called purebreds in the Empire."

"Someone from the royal family?"

"I thought even the Nebulis royal family would waver if one of their relatives was in danger. And the people of the Sovereignty

would be concerned as well. That way, I could make them come to the negotiation table even if they don't want to."

"...Are you telling me you're trying to forcibly start peace talks all by yourself?" Alice knit her eyebrows together and crossed her arms before pressing her fingertips to her glossy lips.

"By your logic, having me as a hostage would force my mother to come to the table to negotiate. But the girl you assisted was a weak mage. She wouldn't have been useful for your cause. That's why you decided you might as well set her free."

Then Alice was silent for a few moments.

"...Fine, that's not inconsistent. If anything, it's persistent." An exasperated smile had formed on her lips. "You're probably not lying, since it's so like you to have this idea... But it won't work. Nothing will change."

"Why?"

"Say you really did take me as a prisoner of war. My mother wouldn't move a finger. That's why there's no room for peace. It's nothing more than a dream. I'm guessing you've never been to the Sovereignty. Of course you wouldn't know how much we despise you there."

The roots of the century-long war ran deep.

Peace negotiations would never be held over one little hostage, purebred or not. The people of the Sovereignty wouldn't allow that.

"...But..." Alice unfolded her arms. "...I didn't know someone like you was in the Empire. I couldn't believe that someone wanted to fight to 'end the battle,' among the terrifyingly barbaric Imperial soldiers. Plus...I've got a good grip on your personality since we spent time together in the neutral city."

The Ice Calamity Witch pointed her finger at him from above the hill.

With that, Aliceliese Lou Nebulis IX made a grand proposition: "You. Become my subordinate."

"Excuse me?" Rin was the one who cried out. "Wait, Lady Alice! Wh-wh-wh-what do you think you're doing?! This isn't what we discussed. We didn't go over this in our meeting last night!"

"I just thought of the idea."

"Outlandish! I mean, to begin, the queen and Elletear and Sisbell would never allow you to have an Imperial soldier working for you! Never!"

"We can go over the details later."

Quiet. Alice put up a level hand in order to subdue Rin.

"I will secure you a position. You'll become a refugee of the Empire," continued the princess with surprising ease. "The Sovereignty will accept anyone who isn't discriminatory toward mages. Especially since you have the strength of a Saint Disciple and know the secrets of the Empire. If you sincerely want to create a world without strife, they will accept you all the more."

She looked right at him. She'd given him an order, but there was a lingering sincerity, eagerness, and hope in her gaze, too.

"I-Iska...?"

He felt the soft touch of fingertips at his back. When he looked slightly to the side, he found the petite captain looking at him. Tears welled in her eyes, and her shoulders shrank from worry.

"Uh, um...so..."

"It's okay." Iska stopped her from saying any more.

"I can't," he answered the princess atop the icy hill. "It's not an issue of remuneration. I can't stand on the Sovereignty's side."

"...And why would that be?" The eyelids of the girl with flaxen hair fluttered.

It wasn't a manifestation of anger but worry.

Ah, of course. I knew you'd react this way. Her voice carried some of her residual fears.

"Tell me why."

"There are two reasons: One, I have family and friends in the Empire. I have friends in my unit and superiors who have treated me kindly. Think about how you have family in the Sovereignty, Alice."

"And the other?"

"There's no possibility that the Sovereignty can negotiate peace with the Empire.

"Say the situation were reversed and you took one of the Eight Great Apostles as a prisoner of war, Alice. If you demanded a peaceful resolution, the Empire wouldn't listen. If anything, the Eight would be happy you got rid of their competition. Unlike your side, Alice, they're all just strangers to one another—not linked by royal blood."

Peace was the only way to stop a century-long war without the complete annihilation of one side. And they could do that only by having the Nebulis Sovereignty accede to their negotiations.

"Yes. That sounds more like the Empire I know. They'll mercilessly toss aside anyone once they are done with them. A collection of humans who don't recognize other humans…" Alice bit her bottom lip.

The magazine in her hands frosted up. Ice started to crawl over its pages.

"You realize what that means, don't you?"

"…I do."

Get back. Iska kept Mismis in check with his left hand and his right swung around to his back. He felt something firm: His fingertips met the handle of his astral blade.

"I can't walk alongside you, Alice."

"……Is that so? In that case, I guess we really are enemies!"

The magazine crumbled to pieces, disappearing into thousands

of shards of ice, records of the past shattering into countless fragments.

This might have marked the moment they decided they were on different sides.

"Capture me—if you can."

But Alice stopped Rin from making a move and covered her face with the headdress from their first meeting in the Nelka forest.

"There's a one-in-a-million chance you'll get me and a one-in-a-billion chance my mother would want to negotiate with the Empire. Who knows? Your dream might just come true."

"You can also eliminate me as you please. You would achieve a step forward in unifying the world, Alice."

" ...... "

" ...... "

The witch hid her face and emotions beneath her headdress.

The Imperial soldier gripped his astral swords in either hand.

Rin and Mismis forgot to breathe as they watched from behind as they were told to stand back.

""*You stubborn idiot!*"" the boy and girl bellowed together.

It was as though their agony had been brought to the surface and carried through the wilderness.

This was an unavoidable future. They should have known the maelstrom that was to become their fate. Their screams strained from their anger and grief, the howls reaching into the distance.

They moved at the same time.

Alice's astral power and Iska's astral swords shrieked in tandem, rumbling with the intensity of a small earthquake.

Their rage shook the entire planet.

"Wha—?!"

They skidded to a stop, just as they were about to charge toward each other.

A gust of cold air emerged from the tip of Iska's sword and shot through his body like a surge of electricity.

...What's happening?

...What was that...insane chill?!

He'd never experienced anything like it before. He'd stood on many battlefields and had brushes with death before, but he'd never sensed such bloodlust.

Iska could feel it filling the air on his skin.

"Rin, what was that just now?"

"...I'm not sure, but my astral power was disturbed by it as well. I can't control it!"

"Wait, I think I can hear something," said the strongest mage of the Sovereignty, stifling her voice and pulling off her headdress. "There's something above— Riiiiiiiiin, get out of the way!"

"Captain Mismis, get back!"

Psht! A fissure opened in the blue skies.

For a moment, it looked as though a black thread had sliced through the air. But then the sky parted to make way for a stormy cyclone.

"Ahhh...!" The captain tumbled over, unable to withstand the wind.

Iska was sure he'd seen something appear in the sky above.

"...The astral sword. The blade that betrayed the planet..."

It was a girl with pearlescent hair, flowing in the wild tempest.

Her lean figure peeked out from a billowing, mottled overcoat. She was tanned brown and looked young. Based on her outer appearance, she couldn't be older than twelve or thirteen.

That was exactly why he was shocked when he heard her.

"Revered Founder?" Alice let slip.

Iska doubted his ears.

"Why is the Revered Founder here when she should be slumbering underground…? No. Why did she awaken…?"

Alice was a direct descendant of Nebulis, and she'd just called this girl the "Revered Founder."

"The Empire…gnaws away at this planet where the astral power resides…like a plague."

From her small, childish lips, she issued a curse, the manifestation of a profound hatred.

"…Ngh."

"You should all simply vanish." The Grand Witch raised a dainty hand.

As soon as they realized what she was doing, Iska and Alice protected their companions and retreated.

There was an invisible explosion.

As though the unseen hand of God had come down, the atmosphere condensed, and an intense shock wave rippled out.

"Wh-what?! What just happened?!"

"I'm not sure. It's just…"

Amid the thick cloud of dust, Iska let go of Mismis. He noticed the cold sweat on his back.

"Captain, take cover behind me. I'm not confident I can beat her."

A dark silhouette stood out in the cloudless sky.

It was the Grand Witch Nebulis. The oldest mage in existence, the one who'd turned the capital into a sea of flames, had just manifested above their heads.

CHAPTER 5

The Founder

1

An hour before this encounter, the royal palace of Nebulis was engulfed in a tremor that was more severe than anything that had come before it. The earth rumbled in a way that seemed to proclaim the end of times. Fissures erupted in the ground. The glass windows in the palace blew out one after another.

"I can feel every bit of astral power in the Sovereignty resonating all at once. What's the meaning of this?"

Queen Mirabella Lou Nebulis IIX followed the underground passageway that continued to quake before entering the ceremonial chamber. Ahead, just down the slope of the natural limestone cave, she could make out two soldiers kneeling on the ground, illuminated by a bonfire.

"What is going on? What could have possibly compelled you to call on me right when we're dealing with this?"

"Ma'am! That's because...!" The two snapped their faces up and pointed behind her.

The queen followed their extended fingertips with her gaze and stopped at the monumental black stone pillar, where the slumbering Founder Nebulis was affixed.

"Have the Revered Founder's bindings come undone?!"

The chain clasps that had wound around her arms and legs were broken into pieces.

"What happened?"

"We don't… The Revered Founder's hand started moving all of a sudden, and—"

"You're saying she tore them off herself. The rumbling must have started around the same time. That's why you called me here," the queen extrapolated.

As the girl with copper skin continued to float in the air, she didn't so much as move an inch. Her head slumped over, and her eyes were still tightly shut, curtaining her pupils. Based on appearances alone, she seemed to be fast asleep.

"……"

The dark-skinned girl slowly began to lift her head.

"*The astral sword*… I feel strong wavelengths of astral power… Are they fighting…?"

She strung together a sentence as though speaking to herself. When she finished, her body flipped over in the air, and an inky, foggy substance started exuding from an astral crest on her back.

"Is that astral power?! Her body is…!"

Her power manifested as jet-black wings, glossy as a dewy feather. They began to flutter gently, though her eyes remained closed.

"Is it going into automatic self-defense mode? O, astral power, are you trying to protect our Revered Founder?!"

The queen had seen how the words *astral sword* had formed on the Founder's lips. Though she didn't know what it meant, she

knew the current state of affairs was alarming—enough of a threat to cause the Founder's astral power to make a defensive move.

"Revered Founder!"

"——**The astral sword…** *You will be returning it…*"

The dewy black wings concealed her body, and the ancient mage vanished as though she had become one with the air.

"Did she disappear?" The guards were dumbfounded.

The queen approached the black pillar, sparing the guards only a backward glance, and touched its rocky surface, the resting place of the Founder Nebulis, with her fingertips.

"…The reason is still unknown. And I did not think we could call on her to rise from her slumber. But if we have her power…" She continued with a cold smile, and she wasn't talking to anyone in particular. "…Then the day of the Empire's defeat draws near."

2

The yellow sand swirled up in a dust cloud, dense enough that visibility was almost nil. When the wind passed through to clear it away, Iska saw a giant gash on the earth with the curvature of a mortar.

It was a crater. The ground had been gouged out, leaving a gaping hole in the soil.

In the past, Iska had seen a rocket blast into an uninhabited wasteland for a training exercise, but that wouldn't even come close to rivaling this destructive power. More importantly—the attack that had caused this was entirely invisible, and he couldn't tell what had happened. And the catalyst of this explosion was just a girl.

"The Founder Nebulis…"

She was a young girl with dark skin and pearlescent hair,

floating high in the sky with something resembling dewy black wings on her back.

"I-Iska? Uh, um… Who is this 'Founder'?"

"I think you already know. The Grand Witch Nebulis has been alive all this time—for a hundred years, back when she caused that incident."

Everything had started when some Imperial researchers discovered this inexplicable source of energy, this "astral power," deep in the earth. It'd taken those humans as hosts and shared its unusual power with them, leading to the creation of the first mages—those the Empire scorned as witches and sorcerers.

…Among them, one girl was showered by the greatest amount of energy.

…Which made her the most feared witch in the Empire at that time.

She'd been persecuted with more fervor than anyone else and eventually became the one to loathe the Empire more than anyone else: the Grand Witch.

"This is so unfair! We've only got the two of us on our team…!" Mismis complained in a trembling voice, pointing at the two mages in front of her eyes.

"The Founder Nebulis…? I can't believe you'd have this legendary witch as backup. Do you think it's fine to do whatever you want now that negotiations have fallen through? Is that how Nebulis does things?"

"W-wait!"

Their eyes met Alice's.

Her glistening blonde hair became disheveled from her frantic reaction. "No! *I didn't do this!*"

"…What?"

"Rin, don't tell me you did?" Alice asked.

"N-no, I didn't. The last time I saw the Revered Founder was

underground with you, Lady Alice. I haven't heard anything about this, even from the queen!" Rin yelled in a hoarse voice.

As she shouted, the pitch-black wings on the Founder's back flapped above her head.

"I manipulate the planet's memories."
"I contact the Will in the third layer. I beckon it to the sur-face of the planet."

Psht. A cleft formed by the feet of the Grand Witch.

The sky that had been pure-blue until that moment cracked into two, splitting as a flickering red *something* peeked its face out of the fissure.

…What is that? Something is appearing out of thin air, just like Nebulis.

…Red. "Beckoning"? No, it can't be.

Shit. With full faith in his own judgment, Iska hollered, "Jump into the crater!"

He grabbed Mismis's hand and pulled her forcibly toward it.

"Hide, Alice!"

"What?"

"You'll be engulfed in flames!" He slid down the slope of the cra-ter with Mismis in hand.

The moment Alice and Rin tumbled down behind them, *that* red thing crawled out from the ruptured space.

It was the astral power of flames. No—that thing far sur-passed what could be considered astral power, gushing with energy incomprehensible to humankind.

"Mow them down."

There was a massive detonation.

As the flames from the astral power seared the atmosphere, the

heat caused the gases to expand, instantly creating a shock wave. Combined with the present oxygen, the attack created a fierce inferno and set off a chain of explosions.

There wasn't any way to escape this hellscape other than ducking into the crater. But even then...

"Holy crap, it's hot!" Mismis yelped as she squeezed her hands over her ears. "This is bad, Iska. The heat is pooling into the bottom of the crater—"

"Close it up," Alice ordered, and frigid winds came at her command, forming a wall of frost that glittered like white gems.

The thin film obstructed the oncoming hot air.

"Lady Alice, why bother protecting them?"

"This isn't the time to argue."

Rin flashed Iska and Mismis a look of suspicion as Alice focused her gaze on the sky beyond the thin sheet of ice, keeping track of the one called the Founder—the one that should have been their ultimate reinforcements. But Iska could see Alice's confusion.

"Her first attack as well as that blast of fire... The Revered Founder is attacking us," Alice observed.

"B-but...isn't it because she saw these Imperial soldiers?"

"It would be unbearable if that's the only reason she attacked the two of us, Rin. I mean, we wouldn't have made it if Iska didn't warn us in time. Am I wrong?"

"...You...you're right." Rin balled her hand into a fist and nodded once. "It's true...that we were saved by an Imperial soldier. I'm guessing the Revered Founder has not recognized us as her brethren—" she answered, kneeling.

"Hold up. That Founder or whatever isn't on your side?" Iska cut her off.

Besides the obvious fact that they were being attacked by the Grand Witch Nebulis, Iska and Mismis couldn't wrap their heads

around what could possibly be going on among the three from the Sovereignty.

"First off, we don't even know if that's actually Nebulis," Iska said.

"Are you seriously doubting that she's real? Even after you've witnessed her power?" Rin glared at him. "The Empire calls her the Grand Witch. In Nebulis, we call her the Revered Founder, the one who established our country."

"Then why attack Alice? Isn't Alice her direct descendant?"

"......" The astral mage of earth swallowed her breath.

The way she averted her eyes made it clear to him that answering his question would mean divulging the Sovereignty's secrets.

"Her astral power is going into automatic self-defense."

"...Lady Alice."

"There's no reason to hide it now that they know the Revered Founder is alive." The princess of Nebulis turned around. "After her battle with the Empire a hundred years ago, the Revered Founder had exhausted her powers and fell into a deep slumber to recover. No one knows the identity of the astral power in her. We call it the 'astral power of time and space,' but that's nothing more than an epithet."

"Astral power that no one knows about, huh..."

"It's been protecting the Revered Founder as she sleeps," Alice continued as though it was completely obvious.

Among astral powers, there were those who would try to protect its human host. Iska remembered hearing that these methods of self-preservation were more visible when a mage's astral power was stronger. But in the Empire, the concept was nothing more than a hypothesis.

"Does that mean Nebulis is still asleep?"

"That's my guess. I don't know what her time-space astral

power responded to, but I believe she's been attacking us indiscriminately because she isn't awake, meaning she can't control it. At least, that's the only way I can make sense of this, but..." The princess choked up.

"This is so frustrating...," she said faintly.

"Frustrating?"

"—"

Her eyes had been locked on the sky until now. For the first time, she turned to face him with bugged-out eyes like a pair of blood moons. Her eyelids snapped wide open, and her ruby irises unblinkingly quavered as she looked wordlessly at Iska.

"I wanted to finish *this thing of ours* with you and me alone." She chewed on her lip.

It was as if she was trying to hold something back. For a brief moment, she couldn't completely conceal her emotions and smiled tearfully at him.

"Ever since we ran into each other in the neutral city, something weird has been building up in my chest... I know this feeling makes me a failure of a princess. I came here intending to end all that—to settle our fight in the Nelka forest, which was cut short. That's why I came in the same clothes as our first battle."

She gripped the hem of her royal gown tightly until it was all wrinkly.

"...I was looking forward to it. I didn't tell my mother about this. I even told Rin she wasn't allowed to intervene. I wanted to settle this with you without anyone else getting in our way. But out of all the things that could happen, that jerk butted in and ruined everything!"

"Th-that jerk?! Lady Alice, you can't speak about the Revered Founder—"

"It's fine. Anyway, we can't continue holing up in here. Let's escape."

Alice snapped her fingers.

The ice film burst and scattered, colliding into the scorching current of air that continued to blow and wreck the wilderness. The two gales seemed to bite into each other as they mixed and canceled out each other.

"Captain, run."

Iska dashed up the side of the crater.

Waiting for him in the air was the Grand Witch, surrounded by scattering embers, still bearing the same emotionless look. She turned her face to them, but her eyes remained tightly closed.

...They're right. She's not conscious.

... What Alice said about her still being asleep is probably the most accurate.

The Grand Witch had felt the presence of an Imperial soldier and automatically launched a counterattack. They could assume that the astral power of space and time had continued to loyally follow the orders of Nebulis for a century, before she'd fallen asleep.

"Revered Founder, I'm grateful that you've come to help, but I would like to settle this with him on my own!" Alice squeezed out. "Revered Founder, please return to the royal palace!"

"—"

The oldest astral mage remained silent. But even though she was unconscious and her head lolled to the side, she seemed to lend an ear to Alice as she remained suspended in the air. However...

"No! You can't, Lady Alice!" Rin grabbed her master's hand and yanked her back.

Rin was a top-class mage who had trained to protect Alice from the earliest days of her childhood. Her finely tuned ability to

sense danger allowed her to read the Founder's movements a split second before she could unleash an attack.

"Does an astral mage dare to get in my way? If you choose to join forces with the Empire..."

The Founder was the oldest mage in existence, bearer of a seething, roiling hatred. Even the words of a fellow mage were nothing more than a faint spray of water compared to her rage.

But Alice hadn't known that.

In other words, the Founder considered anyone who got in the way of her revenge an enemy.

"Begone from this planet!"

A towering flaming sword appeared from the sky, even higher than Nebulis, far up in the heavens.

From the rift above, an inferno in the shape of a blade sliced through the air as it came crashing down. The unbelievable heat it gave off melted the soil. As the fiery hundred-yard sword came closer and closer—

"Lady Alice, get away!"

An earth golem crawled up from a spot by Rin's feet.

Though she was loyal to the Founder, Rin had been suspicious of her motives all along and had secretly prepared this counter-measure just in case.

"Rin?!"

The golem hurled Alice out of range of the impact. That was the last moment she caught a glimpse of Iska, who was holding on to Mismis.

—The massive sword bore into the earth.

The ground all around it turned into lava, while a massive crack opened up along the sword's path, spitting out enormous waves of flame and heat. Embers scattered into the air, starting even more fires.

"Iska! The firestorm is heading toward the city...!" Mismis shrieked with a grim expression as she witnessed the sky of the neutral city burn crimson. "We need to help them fast!"

"Calm down, Captain. It looks worse than it actually is. It's just burning ash. Most of it is gonna drop to the ground and go out. So long as everyone stays calm and handles the situation properly, it won't cause a major fire... If anything, our biggest issue is the opponent in the sky."

They needed to figure out how to deal with their trickiest problem—the Founder Nebulis. Even if they requested help from the capital, they were too far away. They couldn't hope for Jhin or Nene to run to their aid.

Just as Iska was about to say as much out loud, something else caught his eye.

"Rin?! Rin, answer me!"

The attendant was collapsed on the scorched earth. Alice desperately held Rin and shrieked her name. Her golem had crumbled to pieces in front of them and dissolved back to dirt.

Rin had managed to get Alice away from the sword, but that left her no time to escape, so she only managed to take cover in the shadow of the golem. She'd avoided taking a direct hit from the flames, but she couldn't do anything about the heat that suffused the air.

"Rin, please open your eyes..."

"Don't move her around like that."

Iska gripped his black astral sword and stopped Alice from trying to shake her attendant's shoulders. He leaped in front of the two girls.

—A flash of light.

With his black sword, Iska severed and destroyed the second wave of fire aimed at a defenseless Alice. It disappeared, melting into the air.

"That's what your astral power is for."

"What?"

"Use ice to cool Rin down. That's how you treat burns."

"...Oh!" The princess jerked her face up to meet his.

At the same time, a chill seeped out of her fingertips and curled around Rin over her clothes.

"Captain Mismis, take her to the hospital! Better yet, take her to a specialist, an astral power healer!" Iska pointed at the neutral city of Ain, shooting a glance at the falling embers.

"Then alert the city inhabitants. Make sure they do not leave the city walls under any circumstances. From this point forward, this wasteland is going to become the most dangerous battlefield in the world."

"...What? Uh, um..."

"Hurry!"

"O-okay! Be careful, Iska!"

The captain quickly came to her decision and lifted the mage who was supposed to be an enemy onto her back. Then she started running toward the distant city.

Iska didn't watch as she left. He had already turned to stare at the opponent above his head: the Founder Nebulis. The strongest astral mage. The one who had been possessed by her hunger for revenge.

"Nebulis."

Iska held the black astral sword in his right hand and the white in his left—the only pair of astral blades in the world, which his master had entrusted to him.

"One hundred years ago, you might have been the hope that guided every astral mage. But now, you're different. After seeing your actions, I've finally come to a realization. Right now—"

"This era doesn't need you!" yelled out a voice, ringing as if it were a wind chime made of ice—a cry that was strong, clear, and absolutely unwavering echoed through the wilderness. "You call yourself the Founder? Have some shame. No one needs you anymore!"

The one who had uttered those words was the girl standing next to him.

"You interfered when Iska and I were trying to settle things, threatened the neutral city, and even hurt Rin, a fellow mage! …Nebulis, you—and you alone—are a real witch!"

Aliceliese Lou Nebulis IX, the princess who shouldered the burden of the modern Sovereignty, pointed at the architect of her own country.

"Your powers will give birth to nothing. You can't help anyone achieve happiness."

"I agree. You don't know anything about this generation." Iska tried taking a step forward.

"Imperial soldier. Astral mage. You're both—"

""Quiet.""

The Founder was cut off by the boy and girl in perfect unison, speaking to the witch captured in a dream that she refused to wake up from.

"What you are doing is meaningless. It's not the future I want," Iska said.

"It isn't the world I'm aiming for, either."

The two of them understood it in their own way: They were enemies.

The day would come when they would fight each other. But that was for them to settle. They didn't need anyone else butting in.

"That's why—"

""(Revered) Founder, (please) go back to sleep for another century!""

Iska, the Successor of the Black Steel, and Alice, the Ice Calamity Witch, hollered together, back-to-back.

CHAPTER 6

Iska, the Successor of the Black Steel, and Alice, the Ice Calamity Witch

1

Sector Three of the Imperial capital.

Nene looked out the window to see the sun at its peak and used her fingertips to push aside her bangs, which were slick with sweat.

"Phew. It's hottt. It's already noon, too."

The ends of her hair held on to droplets of sweat. She was dressed lightly in thin training clothes. Behind her was a rack of weight lifting equipment.

"Hey, Jhin. You think Iska and Captain Mismis are coming back soon? Training in this room forever is getting boring."

"We're training to protect ourselves. It's not a matter of whether it's boring or not." The silver-haired sniper sat on a metal bench.

He'd already finished his self-training regimen earlier and was starting to perform maintenance on his favorite rifle.

"That's true, but, like, that's not what I was trying to say."

"Are you saying that all four of us should be doing it together?"

"Right! That's it, Jhin. You totally get it!"

"It's fine if they skip a day. We know they're heading over to the neutral city."

"But what are they doing there?"

The night before, the captain had suddenly informed them about the change of plans. She usually didn't try to hide what she was doing or where she was going, but this time, she was strangely ambiguous. When they pressed her on it, she didn't seem to know herself what she would be doing.

"If it has anything to do with our unit, they would have met at the capital. Since they didn't, we don't have any business worrying about it."

"But Captain Mismis went with him, right?"

"......" Jhin gripped the scope that he'd taken off the gun and closed his mouth. He'd gone quiet.

"...Iska *has* been off lately," he answered eventually in a low voice with carefully selected words.

"Off? Why do you say that?"

"Something in him isn't running properly. It feels like his mind and body aren't aligned. He said he hasn't been getting much sleep lately, right?"

"Yeah, ever since we went to the Nelka forest."

"Where he ran into the Ice Calamity Witch." The sniper brought a leg up on the bench before hugging his knee. "And he's been going to the neutral city nonstop since. If someone from the Empire and Sovereignty met there, no one would know. Iska's gone twice, and the third time he's taking the captain with him..."

"Huh? What're you saying? Jhin, did you figure something out?!"

"...No, it's nothing."

"No way! Jhin, you just looked away from me!"

"Ugh, just be quiet already. Come on, everyone around us is staring. We're making a racket—"

A sound came from Jhin's lap—from the communicator on the bench, which suddenly started blinking red and yellow.

"It's an emergency call. And…speak of the devil."

"Captain Mismis?"

"If we're to believe the name on the screen." Jhin stared intently at it before he pressed the receiver to the side of his face. "It's me. I'm with Nene. Yup, training. Of course, if there's anything wrong, we can come right away."

From up close, Nene witnessed the moment his smart eyes opened wide.

"…The *Founder Nebulis*? Wait, calm down, boss. What's going on?" Jhin stood up, still gripping his scope in his hand. "…I understand. Actually, no, I have no idea what's going on, but I get that something is happening over there."

He glanced at Nene from the corner of his eye. From his nervousness, Nene could understand something unusual was going on.

"At the neutral city of Ain, huh. It's too far for Nene and me to get there in time. Who's holding her back…? Iska? He's planning on doing it on his own?"

There was silence.

A moment later, the sniper declared in a firm tone, "In that case, this isn't the time for me or Nene to intervene." He knew Iska the best. "Boss, you should take refuge, too… What? The legendary Grand Witch? Yeah, I know, but it doesn't matter."

"*B-but, Jhin?*"

"If his opponent is a mage, Iska won't lose. Who's going to stop this good-for-nothing war if not him?"

Jhin had absolute conviction as he answered the captain through the receiver.

"That's the whole reason why he's the Successor of the Black Steel."

2

They were on the scorched wastelands.

The neutral city of Ain was still plagued by embers in the background as fire and sandstorms flew about and raced up the hill.

"Imperial soldier…"

The Founder Nebulis continued to float nearly ten yards off the ground. Her eyes were shut tight, and her expression was practically blank, completely devoid of emotion. The dark-skinned girl raised a slender hand into the air as though she were the seasoned conductor of an orchestra.

"Dog of the Empire. Oh, how your kind have oppressed the astral mages."

Her back glowed vermilion from the inside of her lustrous black wings.

"Disappear."

The combusting atmosphere was audible. The moment Iska felt the fire igniting behind him, he sprang from the ground and leaped into the air.

"…You managed to dodge it."

"I didn't."

The Grand Witch's eyebrows knitted together when she realized he had foreseen that she would invoke fire.

Iska immediately denied it. "I did this to face you."

The explosive flames produced a shock wave that pushed him from behind. Using his own jump as a springboard, Iska took advantage of the hot air's lift to launch himself high above—until he wasn't jumping so much as soaring.

"How impressive—using the flames to give you the momentum to leap so far."

He headed into the sky, where the Founder Nebulis waited for him.

...Those dark black wings.

...I definitely saw her wings shining when she invoked her astral power just now.

Those wings radiated with the same color as the *black astral sword*.

They housed the secret to Nebulis's powers. Relying on his epiphany, Iska swung the astral sword up, intending to sever the wings on the Grand Witch's back.

"If you thought your sword would reach me, cool those expectations."

He heard a loud snap, the sound of the moisture in the air between Iska and Nebulis freezing due to astral power.

"Ice?! No way!"

Humans can have only one type of astral power within them. And the Founder had just battered them with intense hellfire moments ago.

...Does she control more than just flames?

...That's strange. She should be able to manipulate only one type of phenomenon.

What kind of astral power did the Grand Witch have?

Even as the glacial wall advanced toward him, threatening to crush him in the sky, his attention was completely dominated by that impossible anomaly.

"Iska!"

A sharp roar cleared his mind.

The call came from none other than Alice, who looked up at him from the ground.

"Hah!"

Iska held his sword sideways and thrust it into the wall,

pivoting around the blade to plant his feet on the thick ice. With that, he hooked the tip of his shoe into a shallow depression and stomped on the wall. As he made his escape, the frost fell to the ground in countless fragments of ice.

However, Nebulis wasn't looking at the wreckage but at the Imperial swordsman who'd escaped unharmed.

"To think you could evade twice."

"I manipulate the planet's memories."
"I contact the Will in the second layer. I beckon it to the surface of the planet."

The Grand Witch snapped her fingers, and the space around her tore open in a vertical gap, which continued to extend down like a twirling tentacle, making its way toward the ocher sand.

...Last time, flames crawled up from that hole.

...Is that about to happen again?

He hunched over and crossed his swords as he readied himself.

Would it be an explosive flame that scorched the wastelands or a supermassive block of ice? Could it be both? He tried to predict the attack to come, imagining countermeasures for each situation in his mind.

However, the oldest mage's powers went beyond his wildest imagination.

There was a rumble at first.

The ground burst open, heaving upward. From the depths of the earth appeared a lion the size of a small mountain.

"A golem?! Does this mean she can invoke the astral power of the earth?!"

"Unfortunately, I don't have the time to fight some rag doll."

Alice kneeled to the ground and touched the shattered crust with her fingertips. "Fly away!" she muttered without waiting for a response.

She'd created a monstrous ice calamity, the same attack she'd used to freeze the Nelka forest. It passed through the ground, rippling as though it were the surface of a tranquil lake and turning the scorched wasteland blue with frost.

She was the mage feared as the Ice Calamity Witch.

When Iska spun around, the ground had become frozen over for as far as he could see.

"I expected nothing less." He landed on the icy slope, where he saw the lion golem frozen mid-roar. "Alice, what's the deal with her astral power?"

"...I'd like to know, too."

Even though she'd just used enough strength to overpower a golem, the Ice Calamity Witch's voice was wispy as she focused on the Grand Witch, who'd been calmly looking down upon them up until that point.

"Even the queen, even my mother, doesn't know anything about her astral power. I thought that if I saw it in practice, I would understand it, but..." The princess ended on a vague note.

Iska was on the same page: He hadn't been able to come up with an appropriate conclusion. The Grand Witch was different from every mage he'd fought so far. Her only abilities should have matched the astral power that resided in her body.

"Do you think it's possible she has multiple?"

"It doesn't seem possible." Alice shut him down. "You know how humans with astral power develop a mark?"

"That's the astral crest, right?"

It was one of the reasons why mages had been oppressed.

A unique mark materialized on the bodies of any who were hosts to astral power. The stronger the astral power, the bigger the mark. *As though they were possessed by demons*—at least, that's what the people who first encountered them feared, which led to the imprisonment of mages.

"I saw her back as she was flipping around in the air. She has tears in her clothes, where the wings are sprouting out, and there's a huge black crest there. That should be where the astral power lies within her, but…" The Ice Calamity Witch narrowed her eyes and stared at the Founder.

"When I saw her in the royal palace, she didn't have those wings. If they're manifesting as a function of her defense mechanism, that means those wings aren't actually a part of her body. They must be formed by the astral power of time and space itself."

"That's all I need to know."

If those pitch-black wings were the embodiment of Nebulis's powers, then as long as he could sever them, he might be able to separate her from her power all at once.

"I need to do something about those wings—"

"**—You—you—you think…**"

"Huh?"

"**—*You think you can do that?*** "The Grand Witch laughed.

It happened incredibly suddenly.

The eyes of the girl with copper skin slowly opened. "…I …remember this place. This is the Vishada wastelands."

"Nebulis?!"

"Oh, astral power. You couldn't have possibly roused me from my slumber for this Imperial soldier, right? I can't fathom why this would be a reason to partially awaken me early."

A light began returning to her eyes, growing sharper by the

moment. "...Hmm, I see. I haven't seen those weapons for quite some time."

The Founder was looking at the astral swords in Iska's hands.

"You know about these swords?"

"__"

She was silent. It wasn't that she had been intentionally keeping information from him: The Grand Witch Nebulis had forgotten to speak, contemplating as she observed the astral swords and Iska.

"Well, it doesn't matter. I don't know how you've acquired them, but those cannot be used by anyone except Crossweil."

"Crossweil?!"

"Does that mean something to you?"

"...That's the name of my master."

He was the strongest swordsman in all of Imperial history, Iska's master, and the previous owner of the astral swords.

...But why?

...Why would a great mage from a hundred years ago know my master?

"You're his...?" The Grand Witch raised one eyebrow inquisitively, but immediately, her small lips curled ominously. "Ha. He baffles me. Why would he entrust the astral swords to a common foot soldier?"

"You won't know unless you fight me."

"It's obvious. There's no outcome in which you could defeat me."

Piercing the ground frosted by Alice's hand, a boiling crimson spray blasted out—magma, the largest source of energy on the planet.

It was molten rock that had formed under extreme heat inside the core of the planet, blazing at nearly two thousand degrees

Fahrenheit. It could eat through city walls and civilian homes, indiscriminately burning and melting everything in its path.

"Can you cross a burning ocean?"

"We'll see."

A jet of lava splashed out as if to engulf him. But amid the intense heat and steam, Iska didn't hesitate to throw himself at the burning spray. He'd intently watched the clumps of magma as they fell back toward the earth and predicted their trajectory. That's why he didn't retreat, surging forward instead, contorting his body as he took one step, then spinning like a top with the next to precisely avoid the molten rock raining down around him. As for the smaller pebbles that he couldn't avoid, he batted them away with the tip of his sword.

"Choosing to fearlessly come closer despite the immense heat, eh?" The girl with tan skin exhaled slightly. "Wrong choice."

The lava that had been spurting up was condensing in midair, transforming into a coiled snake enveloped in fire.

Iska had to crane his head to see the bulky mass that made up the writhing flame golem. At his sides, more free-flowing lava morphed into walls, threatening to close him in. With the fire snake blocking his path forward and a wave of lava slamming into the ground behind him, Iska was being pressed on all sides.

"I have you now, Imperial soldier."

"Hey! Could you stop ignoring me sometime soon?" The boiling lava froze over. "No matter how hot your fires burn, I can hit you right where it hurts."

A curtain of cold air surrounded the girl with golden hair, emanating a blue light. Iska cleared a way for her, and Alice marched forward. Neither of them had put it into words, but the two of them knew exactly what to do.

"...Such a refined chill. Your astral power is of good stock, and you control it well."

"I'm honored to hear that from you."

The frost built up to cover the lava and flame golem. With this scene in front of her eyes, the Grand Witch finally understood Alice's true strength and clicked her tongue in annoyance.

"Girl, I had decided to deal with you after finishing with this Imperial soldier."

"Oh? Aren't you so kind to your fellow mages?"

"It's the opposite." The Founder looked down upon one of her own with a gaze filled with an indescribable cruelty. "A mage joining forces with the Empire… Know that I will not forgive you for your sin, even if you cry and scream for mercy."

"Good. I won't forgive you, either!" The princess returned her ancestor's piercing glare. "You're a mage who's willing to hurt your own people without so much as batting an eye. Look what you did to Rin. You're not a hero to the Sovereignty or to anyone anymore!"

"A hero? How superficial. Something that shallow won't save the world." Her shoulders shook as she chuckled in pity, making it clear she found the idea absolutely hysterical.

"I've known this for a century. This world is full of scars, and it doesn't have anything resembling heroes or a savior. For that reason, I've become a witch—to drive the Empire to extinction. That's all there is to it."

The witch's sneer was filled with bottomless despair. It was a confession of her hopeless anguish.

"I am a witch, and you are my foes."

A ferocious gale began to blow, forming a whirlwind between Iska and Alice that was strong enough to throw someone into the air. It peeled the frost and soil from the ground, and those fragments became a part of the tempest as it grew larger and larger.

"Our astral power formed inside this planet, making it the oldest element on earth. It records all phenomena on this planet, and it

can be called upon from beyond the boundaries of space and time. Now, you eyesores. Disappear to the ends of the world."

"Ngh…"

"Alice!"

As a gust of wind slammed into her from the side, Alice let out a soft cry. The gale had become a raging storm that could blow humans away like scraps of paper. But before she could be whisked off by the roaring winds, Iska grabbed her hand.

With his left sword stabbed into the earth as an anchor, he gritted his teeth as he dug his feet in, pulling Alice back, even as he was exposed to the whipping winds.

—Suddenly, a spray of crimson.

The moment he'd snatched her hand, something had sliced through his arm, spilling fresh red blood.

"Ow!"

"Iska!"

"…You've even got dust devils up your sleeve, huh."

It was as though the wind had turned into tiny blades. This was a supernatural phenomenon that occurred when a tempest picked up gravel from the ground and accelerated it at a terrific speed to be used as a weapon.

"Let go of my hand!" As her body flapped in the wind, the Ice Calamity Witch shouted at him.

As the tempest continued to assail him, Iska's arm began to sprout fresh wounds as cuts turned into gashes that made their way up to his shoulder.

"What are you doing?! Hurry and let go of my hand before your arm tears off!" The mage tried to worm her way loose from his grip.

But he wouldn't allow that.

"…I can't hear you."

"What?!"

"I said that I can't hear you over the wind, Alice! I can't hear you telling me to let go!"

"Ugh." Her face contorted. "…Why?"

Her eyes glittered like jewels, and she looked away.

"…I'm a witch. I'm not someone you should want to offer a hand, especially if you're going to get hurt."

Alice bit on her lip as she gave voice to a thought that pained her deeply.

No matter how ardently she labeled herself a "mage," strangers would call her a "witch," fear her, shun her… She couldn't help but be frustrated.

The one called the Ice Calamity Witch, Alice had bared her soul.

He looked into her eyes.

"Alice." The voice of the Imperial soldier was genial. "Don't you think we're alike in a lot of ways?"

"…Huh?"

"We're both pissed off at her. For your part, Rin got hurt. After getting abused by this mage, I'm in no mood to negotiate with her."

"And what about it?"

"We're not in either the Empire or the Sovereignty. We're in the neutral city. *Our goals are the same.* That's all that matters."

That city had been the beginning of everything. It had been the catalyst.

They'd seen an opera in the neutral city of Ain, gone to the same restaurant, and ordered the same food. Their interests had aligned at a painting exhibition. They'd gotten carried away with all their chatting.

"I feel the same way. I don't want to lose to her, either, so I'm not letting go of your hand."

"......"

Alice opened her mouth as though she had something to say. Then she cast her face down soon after, apparently giving up... But she continued to hesitate and look up, biting her lip over and over again.

"...Can I trust you? Even though you're from the Empire, Iska?" The Ice Calamity Witch's gaze quavered as she asked the question.

Then, in the eye of the raging storm, Aliceliese Lou Nebulis IX's hand glowed.

"Ice Calamity—Myriad of Snow Lights."

Crystals of ice glittered around them as light began to branch out from around her feet and snow blanketed the wastelands in a heavenly scene. It was the embodiment of the word *myriad*: They were surrounded by an uncountable, unfathomable number of icy gems floating through the air, unleashed by Alice's astral power.

"Stars of ice, rise!"

With a flash of blue, the glittering crystals blasted off from the earth's surface and left sparkling afterimages as they flitted into the air. The supercooled shooting stars traced an arc as they hurtled up and over the gale, heading straight toward Nebulis.

"Ice missiles? I didn't think they could overcome this gale... Is that an original technique of yours?" the Founder asked haughtily as she thrust her hands in front of her and condensed the atmosphere itself into a shield.

The strength of her barrier exceeded that of a thick steel wall, and it was impossibly elastic. She brought it up to catch the incoming flashes of ice.

"Ugh!"

Then she fell back.

The feared Grand Witch cast aside her defense and started to take measures to prepare for a retreat. It was a scene that no Imperial soldier could have witnessed a century ago.

"Surely this couldn't..."

A red droplet traced a line down her coppery cheek. The stars of ice had managed to penetrate her shield of air, and one had even grazed her face.

"So it can pierce through my protective barrier."

"I'm far from done. These missiles will keep coming until I use up every last bit of snow on the ground!"

"—"

The dark-skinned girl twirled in the air.

Just when they thought she was about to soar even higher, she suddenly flipped around, turning again as she skimmed the ground before coming to a sudden halt. With her complex and inscrutable flight patterns, she'd skillfully woven through and dodged Alice's barrage.

But Nebulis had managed to evade only a few hundred of these stars at most. Alice chased after her with a web of endless, overwhelming volleys, forcing the Grand Witch to skid to a stop once again. As if to follow suit, the gale that engulfed Iska and Alice settled down as though it had never been there in the first place.

"We've driven you into a corner, Founder."

They'd won. Alice let her confidence in their victory slip into the expression on her face. "Surrende—"

"*So aves cal pile*—Come, divine staff."

"I manipulate the planet's core."

"I connect *my body*. I beckon it from the ends of time and space."

* * *

The Grand Witch turned toward the heavens. A shadow appeared above her head, growing darker and darker as if crowded with clouds. The sun's rays had been interrupted by an ominously black miasmic vortex.

"...My stars!"

The inky current formed a barrier in front of Nebulis, who was still hounded by Alice's ice missiles—but the stars that had once pierced through the atmospheric wall left behind only blue glitter as they ricocheted off the partition.

"What? What is that black stuff?!" Alice rasped as she stared straight up at it.

The air current converged into a vortex, and in the outstretched right hand of the world's oldest mage appeared a pole as long as she was tall.

"It took some time to make this. Apparently my astral power still hasn't fully awakened..."

The black staff twisted and turned while taking shape. The Grand Witch flourished the staff as though she really were a witch performing magic.

"Meet your doom." She threw the staff at them from high above.

When he watched the scene playing out before his eyes, Iska was assaulted by an intense sense of vertigo.

...Is the sky warping?!

...What is this...? What is that creepy staff?!

The staff from the heavens hurtled toward them, and he could feel it in his skin that it was an unavoidable danger.

"Ngh... My stars, take down that staff!"

The staff plunged through the sky as a myriad of ice stars launched from the ground. They crashed together with a

head-to-head collision in midair. Before Iska even realized what had happened, the tip of the divine staff blinked.

—Space itself was completely destroyed.

The air shrieked. The ground roared and broke in two. The endless stream of ice missiles had been so devastated that little remained.

Before he had time to realize it, Iska was blown high into the air by an invisible shock wave.

"...Ugh... Guh, ha...?"

He crashed onto the icy ground and rolled down the slope.

Iska could taste blood in his mouth. He'd probably cut something inside it while falling, but he didn't even know when that had happened. He was completely unaware of when he had been hit by the shock wave.

"...Ali...ce...?!"

"—"

He received no answer.

The princess was lying facedown, unable to raise her head.

He could tell she was breathing as her back faintly moved up and down, but she'd been hit with the shock wave. On top of that, her whole body had hit the ice hard. Whether she was conscious or not, she wasn't in a state where she would have been able to move.

"That's the limit of my divine staff, huh. I guess my powers haven't completely returned after all."

The black staff remained in the air.

Even after it destroyed Alice's ice missiles and then released enough energy to shatter the very ground itself, the Grand Witch still seemed unsatisfied as she snorted.

"...What do you mean, this is *all* it can do...?"

"This is the difference between you and me—the difference that sets apart heaven and earth. Can't you tell?"

Her power was overwhelming, of course. Her gaze told him that they hadn't even been strong enough for her to consider them real opponents from the start. It was true. Alice had barely managed to graze Nebulis's cheek.

Other than that tiny flesh wound, they had done nothing to her. She didn't even have a speck of dust on her clothes.

This was the Founder, the one feared as the Grand Witch, a being who possessed enough power to cause a natural disaster with the wave of a staff.

However.

"___"

"What's that look in your eyes?"

Iska used his astral swords to support himself as he stood.

As she looked down upon him from high above, the Founder seemed unamused as she raised her voice. "You won't run, beg for your life, or look afraid... That gets on my nerves. That impudent manner in which you behold me. Did you dare to think you would successfully stand up against me?"

"No."

He propped himself up with the astral sword in his left hand. Then he thrust the point of the blade in his right hand toward the Grand Witch.

"I'm going to fight you, starting now."

"Are you insane?" Nebulis asked shrilly, as if she couldn't understand a word he said. "The only thing that protected you from the divine staff was that girl's astral power. But take a look around you. She's collapsed and can't even stand up. You have no way of protecting yourself anymore."

"Exactly!" Iska spat blood and kicked at the icy ground. "Alice did all that, so I need to make sure I don't waste this chance."

He'd felt the power of her divine staff in his very bones, but

his body still moved. He ran at his top speed, following along the scarred, broken ground. He sprinted toward the Founder floating with the sun at her back.

"Your only skill is running, you mongrel." The dark-skinned girl pulled the staff toward herself. "Crawl pathetically along the ground."

She waved the staff.

The sky rumbled as though it were about to weep, and the atmosphere warped. A blade fashioned from the space-time continuum came into being with an edge sharper than steel and invisible to the human eye.

But the astral sword that Iska brought down split through the Founder's approaching blade.

"What?"

"Even if it's invisible, I can still sense it."

He could feel the undulation of the warping atmosphere on his skin and listened for the sound of the invisible blade slicing through the air. Even if it was a means of attack he'd never seen before, as long as it was astral power, he could intercept it with his black astral sword.

...That is why I trained.

...So that I will never hesitate, no matter what kind of mage I face.

"What kind of joke is this?"

"Joke? I'm always serious!"

Blades of condensed air rained down on him from all directions.

As he faced the barrage, Iska chose not to retreat or stop but to go faster. The air practically shrieked as he sliced through it with his sword to ward off the invisible blades.

He dodged one that came at him from behind and slipped past another coming from his side. His cheek was grazed and a gash appeared on his shoulder, but Iska wouldn't stop.

"...Keep...running!" The princess scrambled onto her trembling knees. "Rise up."

The ice on the ground started to twist heavenward and transformed into a glacial wall. Bit by bit, it was chipped away as she masterfully sculpted it into a polished staircase right before Iska's eyes. It pointed straight into the sky—a final glittering path of ice that led directly to the Founder Nebulis.

"Here I come."

"How impudent!" The Grand Witch wielded her staff sideways. "You, someone who doesn't even know the true extent of the Empire's countless evils, would dare to face me—"

"You still don't understand, huh." Iska sprinted up the ice stairs. "This pointless war won't end, because people like you are trapped by their hatred!"

"Silence!" She released the powers from her staff. "Astral sword or not, you won't be able to endure this attack!"

Her technique that used the astral power of time and space could wreck the atmosphere and cause the wind to howl. Even if the astral sword could intercept all other astral powers, it was useless against this. The moment the tip of his sword and the point of her staff made contact, it would detonate the very fabric of existence itself. Even if he managed to hack through her staff, he would still get caught in the blast.

"I know. I saw what happened with Alice's missiles."

Shling. The black astral sword rang shrilly as it fell to the ground. Iska had let it drop out of his own right hand.

"What are you planning?!"

"I know what the strongest shield in the world is."

He thrust out his right hand, revealing something broad and flat. It was an "ice seed."

*　　*　　*

"An invincible shield*: It's even resisted the firepower of Imperial weapons of mass destruction."*

She'd said it was invincible.

And Iska chose to believe her—that she'd entrusted him with a shield that could withstand the force of the divine staff.

"Alice!"

When he called down to her, the Ice Calamity Witch replied with just one word as her face remained planted on the ground. Even then, she had absolute confidence in herself.

"…Bloom!"

The shard of ice in his hand burst open, emitting a sharp ringing sound that echoed into the backdrop. The ice seed sprouted into the most beautiful mirror shield in the world—an ice flower.

Though his black sword could sever any astral power, this was the one exception. Aliceliese Lou Nebulis IX possessed the astral power of ice flowers, and its true form manifested as a blossom of frost.

"…Can I trust you? Even though you're from the Empire, Iska?"

While they were swept up by the gale, Iska hadn't let go of her hand. And as their fingers interlaced, Alice had entrusted him with her biggest secret, an ice seed—which bloomed to become Iska's shield.

The most beautiful petals of ice in the world caught the blow of the divine staff.

"That's impossible!"

The witch's staff and the flower of frost groaned before they

both shattered into a thousand pieces, leaving the copper-toned girl exposed and totally defenseless. She couldn't move. Though it was true that her powers hadn't completely returned yet, she was shaken that her ultimate attack had been stopped.

But she seemed to be in a stupor, as if she refused to accept the truth.

"...Why...?"

"Don't you get it?" Iska twirled the white astral sword with his left hand. "A hundred years ago, you'd only take up battles with swordsmen. But you've never had to fight a swordsman *and* a mage at once."

Nebulis had once represented hope for all astral mages. If she'd still been the symbol of change in this era, the battle would have ended on a different note, and Alice wouldn't have entrusted the ice flower to Iska.

But Alice's astral power had come to a decision: The Grand Witch wasn't going to be the mage to shoulder the burden of bringing about the new age.

"Go back to sleep, Nebulis." Iska brought down his sword, aiming at the base of the pitch-black wings that peeked out from the back of her cloak. "Next time you wake up, I bet the world will be in a better place."

There was a tiny cry.

And with that, the girl lost consciousness as the connection to her source of power was severed, falling forward with her eyes shut tight into a deep slumber once more.

Her body was swallowed by a crevice in the sky and disappeared from sight.

INTERMISSION

In This Dark Dusk

The stage was the Imperial capital Yunmelngen around sunset.

As the city was steeped in an intense crimson haze, an event transpired deep underground. Nearly three miles down from the crust of the earth, the dark assembly hall echoed with applause.

"**Brilliant.**"

"**I cannot feel the astral power of the Grand Witch Nebulis. It's all but disappeared, which means he's successfully neutralized her powers.**"

"**It is a pity that we have no images of this battle. Her astral energy was born from the deepest depths of this planet. If we'd gotten our hands on a picture, I'm sure our research would have progressed by leaps and bounds…**"

"**No. There is great meaning in having stopped the Grand Witch's awakening.**"

"**Of course** *that man*'**s successor was the one to do it. Well, well. The results of the battle were just as we'd expected.**"

There wasn't a single light fixture in the room, but it was dimly illuminated by the eight monitors that surrounded a round table,

featuring the silhouettes of men and women. Their physiques could be made out from the indistinct outlines on the screens.

They were the executive body that decided the will of the Empire—the Eight Great Apostles.

"**The Grand Witch has been silenced once more, though the Ice Calamity Witch is still of great concern...**"

"**It's the mission of the Successor of the Black Steel to bring down the witch. If anything, he'll eventually do it for us whether he wishes to or not.**"

"**Indeed.**"

"**The fifth Saint Disciple—Risya In Empire's 'experiment' is also going smoothly. Now that the Grand Witch is asleep, *the Nebulis Sovereignty will fall.***"

"**The man—the Black Steel Gladiator Crossweil—hid the secrets of the planet from us. It seems his successor knows nothing, and our guess was off the mark, but I suppose that's fine. The prophecy of the people of this planet is fast approaching... We're almost there.**" It was the lyrical voice of a woman, mixed with a wry chuckle—a bewitching, intelligent voice, coolheaded enough to plant seeds of fear in those who dared listen.

"**Iska, the Successor of the Black Steel. Your wishes will come true.**"

"**Yes. We will grant you everything you wish. If you wish for peace, we promise you will have eternal world peace.**"

"**—Once we've exterminated every last witch and sorcerer.**"

"**Because that's what this planet wishes.**"

That was the final word. All at once, the silhouettes disappeared from the monitors. With a veil of silence hanging over the Imperial Senate, the only thing that lingered was a faint echo of that applause from earlier.

EPILOGUE

Under This Beautiful Night Sky

Eddies of yellow sand drifted through the wasteland. The ice had melted, revealing the raw gashes gouged into the earth by the divine staff. The wind nudged loess into these dark abysses, filling the earthen pockets slowly, as if the planet were healing its own wounds—as if the planet were moving of its own volition.

"……" Iska cast a sidelong glance at the scene, taking his time to climb up a tall hill. "…It's already so late in the day."

The sandy nighttime breeze grazed the back of his neck, causing him to shiver slightly. He had arrived at the neutral city of Ain at noon, but now he noticed that the sun was fast sinking below the horizon.

Iska walked across the wastelands and walked and walked and walked.

He trudged forward on the desolate earth—nary a light nor road in sight.

"Sorry to keep you waiting."

At the peak of the hill waited a captivating girl with flaxen hair, hugging her knees. She'd finished treating her wounds all by herself as she anticipated his arrival on the dune.

"I think you already know, but it seems like Rin is gonna be all right. She's going to have scars from the burns for a while, but they'll heal naturally over time."

"Uh-huh."

"Jhin and Nene are waiting for Captain Mismis, so she said she's gonna hop on an overnight bus to get back to the Imperial capital as soon as possible. Can she tell them about the whole situation with the Founder?"

"I don't mind. It makes no sense to hide it from them, since she put the neutral city in danger. The Sovereignty takes responsibility for its actions." The princess nodded to herself as she continued to cradle her knees. "I have one thing to say to you, too. I've given it a lot of thought, and I think the Grand Witch must have returned to the underground sanctum."

"In the Sovereignty?"

"Yes. Of course, I can't tell you all the details, but I'll take on the task of watching over the sanctum. I'll have my mother relinquish the keys to the entrance to me, too…and prevent the witch from waking up once again." Alice brushed flecks of sand off herself as she stood up.

Even though she'd sustained injuries all over her body during the fight with the Founder, she maintained a noble bearing—all while looking absolutely breathtaking.

It was just like the first time he'd seen her in the Nelka forest.

"Well then, I suppose that's all we needed to tell each other."

"Yeah."

"…Right. Then let's start again—our final battle between just the two of us."

No one could get in their way, here and now. The spot was perfect. Everything was ready.

Iska, the Successor of the Black Steel. Alice, the Ice Calamity

Witch. Two heroes born in opposing nations, the Empire and the Sovereignty.

Their first fateful encounter started it all, and they'd reached the point where they needed to settle everything now.

"No holding back," Alice warned.

"Yeah."

Alice took a step forward. Iska followed her lead.

"……"

"……"

They each silently watched their opponent as they took another step, then another.

Twenty feet separated them, and then ten.

Ten feet became three.

Before they realized it, Iska and Alice were standing close enough to touch each other.

"There's something I want to say," the Imperial swordsman admitted.

"What a coincidence." The girl of the Sovereignty nodded.

Then—

"…Let's have a truce. Today…I'm too exhausted…," he said.

"…No objections here."

At the same time, Iska and Alice collapsed onto the waste-lands.

"…But it's just for today, okay?" she said.

"I know."

"We're enemies again starting tomorrow, okay?"

"I guess we are."

"……"

"……"

They both looked up at the stars overhead.

"The sky is beautiful tonight."

"Yeah."

They continued to sprawl out next to each other, not moving a single muscle.

If a bird soaring in the night sky peered down at the two, it might have mistaken them for lovers or siblings.

"I can see the 'cradle.' Its constellation is clear tonight. This is the only time of year that it's visible, so this might be the last we'll see of it."

"Which one?"

"That one. You can tell at a glance."

She copied the boy pointing with his finger by raising her own to stretch out into the starry sky.

"The streetlights in the Imperial capital are too bright. I don't get to see the stars that often. Is it that string of blue stars?"

"No, not that one but next to it... No, this time you've missed it completely."

"...It's hard."

"Oh, you're so silly."

They might be enemies. They might be opponents at daybreak, posed to fight each other once more.

But just for that moment, their laughter rang through the air.

Iska, the Successor of the Black Steel, and Alice, the Ice Calamity Witch, continued to look up together toward the star-filled sky.

This is the story of the battle with a witch—a fight between you, a witch, and me. Will we meet next in a distant battlefield? Or a last crusade for the rise of a new world?

Our story has only just begun.

Afterword

This is a story of two enemies and rivals on the battlefield—the main character and the heroine. I guess it's been...about two whole years since the earliest version of this storyline? Now that I think about it, it took me a very long time to finish this book.

During those two years, I was busy writing this novel, deciding on an illustrator (to be mentioned later), and struggling to come up with a title. The deadline started to catch up to me before I knew it, and now I'm three hours away from the cutoff for this very afterword.

It's a sprint to the finish line. I'm panicking right now...

With that said, I'd be grateful if you could bear with me for a while as I elaborate on the story.

Hello, it's nice to meet you. I'm the author, Kei Sazane.

Thank you for picking up a copy of *Our Last Crusade or the Rise of a New World*.

It's been a while since I've published a new book with Fantasia Bunko, even though I made my debut as an author with this imprint.

I worry that you'll berate me for slacking off, but I hope you find it in you to forgive me... As I wrote in my preliminary remarks, I was focusing on creating this book.

(Side note: I've also been working on another series called *Encore: Records of the World's End* with a different publisher under their imprint, MF Bunko J.)

That said, two years with nothing to show for it. That's a long time, now that I look back.

In my line of work, I find it difficult to feel the seasons passing by, since I'm usually hunkering down in front of some manuscript. But during that time, my friends have switched jobs, and my environment has changed, and I've put out several books under another imprint, as I've mentioned before.

If I look at it from a different perspective, I'm thankful that I could let the concept of this book simmer and develop over that time.

With the help of Editor K, I was able to follow a publication scheme, and we made sure to prioritize the quality of the work in front of you.

That said, the release date is drawing near. As I'm writing this afterword, I'm more edge-of-my-seat nervous than happy. I've been losing sleep these days... (I think on the release date, I'll be half-conscious from the nerves.)

Now then, how did you like the book?

The main character and heroine are heroes from enemy countries and rivals on the battlefield. But the ball starts rolling when

they run into each other on the streets, and they realize their relationship is something more than competitive. That's the linchpin of this story.

The main character, Iska, and heroine witch, Aliceliese.

At times, they clash viciously, and at others, they join forces. What is their destiny? I hope you'll anticipate how the series progresses.

And of course, I have to mention the illustrator who enhanced the story. (One might consider the illustrations the main appeal of this book.)

Starting with character design to the cover to the inserts and interior art, I was so excited to see what Ao Nekonabe would come up with. These illustrations are an indispensable part of the book.

I'd like to take this opportunity to thank you, Ao Nekonabe.

I was particularly blown away by the cover. I could feel passion radiating off Alice, and it set the mood perfectly for this story. I'm completely filled to the brim with gratitude, and I'm looking forward to working with you in the future. (And the second volume, which is already underway.)

I'd like to use this space to express my appreciation to another individual: Editor K for managing this book.

I was able to finish this volume because you gave me strength. You were always the first to read my drafts and point me in the right direction. I am thankful to you from the bottom of my heart.

If I wrote down all the instances when you've helped me, I'd go far past the space allotted for my afterword, so I'll refrain from spilling every little thing. But from asking Ao Nekonabe to come on as the illustrator to mulling over the title with me until late into the night, I'd like to thank you... I hope to continue working with you in the future, as well.

*   *   *

And now, I'd like to mention future developments.

To kick things off, this first volume is being published on the same day as the July edition of *Dragon Magazine*, which has a feature and short story on *Our Last Crusade or the Rise of a New World*.

It's based off the original plot with Iska and Alice as the main characters, but this short story will feature new content, intended for those who may be curious about the book. I hope those of you who buy *Dragon Magazine* will read through them.

Next, regarding the second volume.

I've already written the manuscript, and I'm happy to tell you the release date of the next installation here.

Our Last Crusade or the Rise of a New World, Volume 2 is expected for publication on July 20, 2017.

I'm very happy that I'll be able to publish the second volume just two months after the first one. It also nudges and motivates me to try my absolute hardest.

When this book hits the shelves, I'm guessing that I'll be battling against the clock to make the deadline for the afterword in the second volume. (I'm just not used to writing these.)

So there you have it. I don't have many pages left.

Before I end this, I'd like to say that I am thankful for those who picked up this book and stuck with me until this point.

This is the story of the swordsman Iska and witch Alice—at times, a tale of rivals; at others, a boy-meets-girl romance.

Where will their destinies lead?

It would make me happy if you continued to support these two.

*   *   *

So now, then. I hope we'll meet again in the second volume in July.

Written from me to you on a chilly morning early in spring,

Kei Sazane

* I may be able to make more announcements about my books on Twitter. Please check it out if you'd like: https://twitter.com/sazanek

Iska gets insanely stubborn once he's made up his mind.

shoot
y eyes
—no
m.

Nene Alkastone

The mechanic of Iska's unit. She's a cheerful girl who thinks of Iska like an older brother.

n Syulargun

niper of Iska's unit. He and
hare a history of training
the same master.

Think of me as an older sister, and tell me everything!

Mismis Klass

The commanding officer of Iska's unit. She's petite with a baby face, but she's a full-fledged adult at age twenty-two.

If I give up here, who's gonna stop this war?!

Iska

A young soldier who is a part of the imperial army. He was the youngest boy in the Empire to rise to the title of Saint Disciple, which is given to those with the greatest military potential. He wields unique weapons called astral swords.

Our Last Crusade or the Rise of a New World

White steam floated from the surface of the tub, which was filled to the brim with milky, hot water from the jowls of a lion-shaped basin filler. Flowers of all colors danced around various herbs in the water.

"…"

In the bath, Alice put her hand to her ample chest, the sight of which made Rin jealously call her an early bloomer.

There, she could feel her heartbeat, pounding in a way that was puzzling even to her.

It beat faster: *Ba-dump*, *ba-dump*, *ba-dump*. Instead of settling down, it pounded with more force.

"Ugh, what's wrong with me? This is no good! I need a break!"

Rin Vispose

Aliceliese's confidante and maid. She commands the astral power of earth, and she's well versed in the art of assassination.

I coul
with n
closed
proble

Jhi
The
Iska
unde

Keep the events of this day buried deep inside you, Lady Alice.

I won't let anyone get in the way of my goal to defeat the Empire and unite the world.

Aliceliese Lou Nebulis IX

The second eldest princess of the Nebulis Sovereignty. She is a formidable mage with the astral power of ice. She is feared as the "Ice Calamity Witch" by the Empire.